# What Is Said In The Dark

## A Novel

## By

## Tony Hockley

*"What you have said in the dark will be heard in the daylight, and what you have whispered in the ear in the inner rooms will be proclaimed from the rooftops."*

**Luke 12:3**


*"I say a murder is abstract. You pull the trigger and after that you do not understand anything that happens."*

**Jean-Paul Sartre "Dirty Hands" Act 5 Scene 2, 1948**

# Prologue

## Tangier Morocco November 1959

*There was a noise, a click, a shuffle, then stillness; just the wind, he thought – a desert wind, unseasonably hot, rustling the branches of the olive trees. It had broken his reverie; he turned his head on the pillow and shifted slightly in the narrow bed.*

*"All my life, every decision I've made, every step I've taken, false or true, has brought me to this, just like you. Every step you've taken, every corner you've turned has brought you to me. It's not your fault, and it's not mine. Let's just call it fate, can we? Can we?"*

*The figure eased his bulk from the narrow bed and smoothed his oiled black hair back across his elephantine skull. He lit a cigarette and stood for a while in the centre of the mean little room, looking down at the sheet, at the form shrouded in thin cotton, shivering there, despite the cloying heat. Then he leaned down and tentatively patted the boy, who shrank from his touch, giving forth a growl, or a mewl more like. Something animalistic that made the man wince. He scowled, his face creasing above the born- to- hang mono-brow that marked him like a scar. He pulled his trousers up and walked from the room heading along the corridor to the stairs. He noted the blood on his knuckles, and thought about the possibility of blood on his heavy cock. He'd have to wash before joining the man at the hotel bar.*

*The boy waited. He waited until every sound had diminished, even the echo of the man's leaden tread. He lay for a long while, tangled in the sheet, and then he rose, naked, and walked into the cramped and windowless bathroom. He stood before the small foxed mirror and stared at his reflection in the glass. He picked up Maurice's straight razor and opened the blade. He could hear the sound of laughter coming up from the bar on the floor below, male laughter, boisterous, deep and throaty. Logan Frazer and the other one, Frazer holding court as usual. It was this sound, ringing in his ears, that heralded his departure, a rabid cacophony of jackals, mocking him as he travelled, destitute, along the highway.*

# Chapter One

## Soho London Winter 1959

It was that period between Christmas and New Year when the West End of London teemed with hollow eyed consumers, gambolling the length and breadth of Oxford Street seeking bargains and one last throw of the festive dice. Yet just a few yards to the north lay Fitzrovia, and to the south Soho, where other pleasures were to be found for those of a more dissolute bent. It took a singularly resolute individual to hold the line between these two worlds. We find him, gazing forlornly from the window of his room, which sits haphazardly above a bookshop on the Charing Cross Road. Detective Chief Inspector Rake had been having a difficult time of it.

*Another bad morning on the lavatory, that porcelain shriving pew, where remorse and recrimination stare up from their watery hutch, delivering the verdict. Like most people I can deduce the state of my health from the state of my stool, and the state of my stool assailed my every sense with unremitting disapprobation. Attempting to flush away my melancholy along with the detritus of a wilfully debauched evening, I wrapped myself in coat, scarf and trilby and headed to the stairs.*

Cyril Rake, christened in honour of a father he never knew, lost at Gallipoli in 1915, one of one hundred and fifteen thousand dominion troops to perish among those rocky outcrops on that desolate peninsula. Stepping onto the street he took in a lungful of fetid, smoggy London air. He coughed, took a Craven A from his pocket and lit it, exhaling smoke and ghostly vapour into the already darkening afternoon. Pulling the collar of his black Crombie up around his raw-boned neck he walked to Sutton Row, along Soho Square and down Greek Street to the Coach and Horses. The landlord, Norman, greeted him by setting a Whisky Mac on the bar. Rake looked around the room.

"Quiet," he said.

"They knew you were coming," said Norman, turning back to speak with another lost soul sitting further along the bar.

Rake downed his drink and walked to the door, turning as he pulled it open he took a long look round the narrow room.

"If you see Deakin, tell him I'm looking for him."

"I won't be seeing him, he's lost his tab. Try Muriel's."

"Right you are, Norman."

"Not paying for the drink then?"

Rake let the door shut on the rhetorical question and walked along Old Compton Street then headed north up Dean Street towards The Colony Room. He waited on the street until three, when the club would open, nodding at the several men he knew that had likewise wandered to the door from the various hostelries that dotted the area. At five past the hour he made his way up the wretched, foul smelling stairs and entered the club. Muriel Belcher sat on a high stool at the bar whilst her girlfriend Carmel chatted animatedly to a couple of men, who had clearly been granted ingress before the opening proper. The heavily painted green walls always left Rake feeling as though he were in a tropical fish tank, and the atmosphere had a depressing effect on him, especially when he was sober and the place was quiet. He knew it wouldn't be quiet for long when the painter Francis Bacon turned from his conversation with Carmel and shrieked a libidinous "Hello", to a young man who had followed Rake into the room. Muriel looked down her hawkish nose, examining Rake as if he were a specimen.

"Members only, dreary," she purred.

"I am a member, Muriel, as well you know."

"Well then Lottie, open your beanbag and we'll all have a drink. Liven up children, the law's in town. We've got a few pansies in this afternoon Sergeant; I hope you're not here on official business."

"I've just dropped in for a recreational tipple, Muriel, and I'm not a Sergeant. What can I get you?"

"Oh Sergeant, I couldn't possibly be seen drinking with the likes of you."

"Fair enough."

"It sounds like a song doesn't it? Oh Sergeant.... Gilbert and Sullivan, I'll have my usual, bless you."

Rake moved to the bar and nodded a swift hello to Ian, the barman. He ordered Muriel's usual and a large Scotch and water for himself. The room filled, customers that knew who he was gave him as wide a berth as was possible in the cramped space. Soon the club was hazy with smoke and clamorous with trilling laughter and empty badinage, Bacon's voice always to the fore, high-pitched and effusively didactic on any and every given subject. He moved along the bar and stood next to Rake, they nodded a mutual acknowledgement.

"Haven't seen you around here for an age, dear. Are you well?" asked the painter. His convex face looked to Rake like the reflection one might see on the back of a serving spoon, his bow-lipped mouth wet and somehow suggestive and lascivious.

"I'm waiting for Deakin," said Rake.

"He hasn't been about since Christmas, I heard he was feeling seedy."

"Really, what's been the problem?"

"Oh, speak of the devil, you can ask him yourself."

A small, bedraggled waif of a man had swung into the room, brushing past Muriel with a begrudging wave, ducking his head as if to make himself even smaller, or to evade a cuff round the ear.

"Where do you think you're going, cunty?" she howled, causing every head to turn.

"I have an appointment with Mister Rake," he said without meeting her eye, hustling along the bar and leeching onto Rake's sleeve. He leered up at the policeman.

" Gin, double, ice."

"You smell of bleach," said Rake, lifting his face as if slapped.

"Those bastards at The Golden Lion tried to poison me. Here, you should go and bloody arrest them; I was coughing up blood, blood mind you. They fed me Parazone for Sancerre. I intend to sue."

"You should."

"I intend to, I need a gargle."

Rake ordered Deakin his gin and had another Scotch to be sociable.

"Have you missed me Rakey? I've missed you. I had a miserable bloody Christmas, you know. I could have been dead and no one would have noticed. David was away with his people and no one came to see me, not even on Christmas day. Every bugger in London was away, in the country, or so they said. I don't believe them, would you? I don't, I could have laid there dead and been eaten by the ruddy dog, not that anyone would care. David wouldn't care, be glad to see the back of me. Well fuck him, I sold most of his first bloody editions, so he'll probably strangle me anyway, good riddance they'll all say," he took a breath and downed his drink. "Bloody good riddance."

"Ian, another one for Deakin, please."

"It's all about the consolations, Rakey, I've come to realise. All about the fucking consolations, the little pleasures. The little pleasures that life throws your way. Happiness isn't something you find, it's a door you leave open as you wend your way through the streets and alleyways, don't you think?"

"I don't think about it."

"Anyway, where were you?"

"I was working, Deakin."

"Oh, are you on a case?"

"I'm on several cases, one in particular, the Kensington murder."

Deakin nodded sagely, but his head sunk into his shoulders like a tortoise that had had its nose tapped by a twig. If anyone had been interested in talking with him, Rake knew that Deakin would have joined another clique in that moment. Rake gripped Deakin's arm and leaned in, despite the bleach-laden breath.

"The Kensington murder", Rake said again, more emphatically. "Logan Frazer, the impresario. You knew him didn't you? Don't be coy, Deakin, after all."

"After all what? I know a lot of people. Anyway, who said murder? He died in a fire, didn't he?"

Rake drank off his whisky and tilted the glass at Ian Board, the barkeep. The drink was replenished as Deakin downed his gin and proffered the glass, which was iced and topped up. Rake took a sip, savouring the liquor.

"Well, there was a fire, but he didn't die in it."

"Oh really Mister Rake, don't be mysterious. It said in the Sketch he died in a fire."

"And it'll say in the Sketch on Tuesday that he didn't. How well did you know him?"

"I'm never sure whether you're working or gossiping, chief, do you even know the difference yourself?"

"There's a world of difference, John; I just thought you might be able to help me, informally."

"Informally as opposed to what?"

"Formally, under caution."

Deakin looked up and into Rake's eyes. They held each other's stare until Deakin looked back at his drink. He nodded his head slowly up and down, then slid his glass towards the policeman. Rake ordered a refill and lit a cigarette. The room was now crowding about them and someone had started playing the plonky, ill-tuned upright. Deakin started to hum along tunelessly.

"Well?" said Rake.

"I don't like being leaned on, so elucidate or buy me another drink - or fuck off."

"I just want to know something about the man, something beyond the whispers I'm hearing, some detail. I thought you might be able to help me out."

"I'm not a bloody squeaker."

"Well, I pay you money and you tell me things."

"Not this time. I don't know anything."

Rake slid a pound note along to Deakin's elbow and shuffled it against his sleeve. He looked at Deakin and inclined his head.

"I'll be at Gennaro's at eight," he said. "If you want to eat and have a chinwag you can join me. If not there will be a black Wolsey parked up outside your billet with a nice Detective Sergeant called Sweet waiting to bring you along to the Row. Up to you." Deakin took the note and squirrelled it away in his voluminous coat. Rake nodded to Ian and walked towards the door. Muriel tipped her shoe as he passed, catching him on his thigh.

"Aren't you taking little Miss weasel with you, Sergeant? She's outstayed her welcome."

"He's got money Muriel, let him spend it here, might as well."

Muriel Belcher lifted her imperious gaze and looked Rake in the eye; the slight lift to her mouth was almost flirtatious.

"You look tired Cyril, how are you, really?"

"I'm fine, I don't much like Christmas if I'm honest, you know, as things are."

"You could have popped round, dear. We did a nice lunch. You'd have been welcome, you know that."

"I'm not much company at the moment, but thank you Muriel, I mean it."

"We would have managed, anyway, pop by later if you feel like seeing in the New Year with a few old friends. It'll be a bit lavender, but you won't mind that."

"I'm not sure I'd be welcome, things move on."

Muriel leaned in and planted a light kiss on the detective's cheek, and then she dragged on her cigarette and plumed smoke up towards the ceiling.

"Happy New Year, Cyril, let's hope nineteen sixty lifts the lid." She saluted Rake with her drink as he headed through the door to the stairs and the dark street beyond.

Sleet was falling spitefully as Rake stepped onto Dean Street and wended his way back to the Charing Cross Road. He walked the few yards along the familiar alleyway that led to his door and climbed wearily up the stairs to his flat. The living room was as cold as a dead man's hand so he kept his coat on and flipped the electric fire into life. It ticked for a few minutes and then the filaments began to glow red and the ticking slowed and softened. He looked over at his bed, hastily made in the small hours of morning, and thought about getting back in between the blankets. But he disliked the feeling of waking with night still stretching out before him and a hangover in the offing, so he wandered into the kitchenette and made coffee. His tinnitus was playing its discordant tune so he switched on the radio, which hummed for a minute before a warm voice came comfortingly into the room. Rake sat, still in his overcoat, and drank his coffee. He felt ill at ease, uncertain whether to ring Ruth, unsure which would be the more meaningful, to ring or to hold his counsel on this, the last night of the decade. At seven forty he came to from a reverie and washed the cup and the teaspoon, laying them on the draining board, where they would await his return, a phenomena with which he was still getting acclimatised, Ruth being a neurotic tidier. He clicked the fire off, but left the radio and his desk lamp on, so as to be welcomed on his return, by at least some semblance of life. Then he headed back to Dean Street, to Gennaro's, and to Deakin.

Rake had booked his usual corner table, and he sat, dipping his crust in the large glass of Chianti that perched on the starched white linen before him. The restaurant, always busy, was now thronged with merry hordes of celebrating, inebriated couples and noisy cliques, many of who were known to the detective. He looked at his watch, it was just past nine, so reluctantly he waved a waiter to the table and ordered a dish of Vongole and a second bottle of wine. He was still picking at the spaghetti when Deakin crashed into the room. He weaved his way to the table, calling hellos to the people he knew, and to the people he didn't know, being ignored by all - except for one large blonde fellow, who swore at him. He sat, still in his British Officers Warm, which was stained and crested with cigarette burns. He tore off a hunk of bread, wiped it through Rake's food, and ate, washing the bolus down with Chianti. Beckoning a waiter he ordered food, then took another swipe through Rake's sauce and sat back, grinning mischievously. He was very drunk.

"Alright if I get some lovely gin?" He licked his lips, his big tongue purple with wine and with life. Rake nodded and Deakin ordered a double gin, raising the glass in a salute.

"So?" he said.

"You talk, I'll listen, and then we'll see."

"You first. Was it a fire or not?"

"The fire was set post mortem, no smoke in his lungs apparently, so they had a proper look. There were fractures to the skull, they'd put it down to a fall, but he was bludgeoned to death it seems."

"The infamous blunt object."

Deakin's meal arrived and he spun his fork through the pasta and took in a mouthful. He spoke through the food.

"Who's in the frame, Fabian?"

"I'm not here to be pissed about, John. Paint me a picture." Deakin held up his hand and focused on eating, washing the food down with Rake's Chianti. Rake was a patient man; he lit a cigarette and sipped at his wine. Deakin mopped up sauce with a crust, belched appreciatively and lit one of Rake's Craven A.

"Logan Frazer," he said. "Mister Music, the biggest cunt on Tin Pan Alley, biggest player since Larry Parnes Shillings and Pence. Logan ran his own stable of Dilly boys and northern knuckleheads from offices on the Strand. He had a stake in a couple of West End shows, and the wrestling down in Catford and Lewisham. He was known as the Fagin of Soho. Had number one hits with a couple of the boys, Deacon Blood and Little Mickey Magnet, remember him? He was a talent, Roy Huff that was his real name. Ring any bells?"

"Carry on."

"What do you mean?"

"Lift some stones."

"He was a ponce."

"Roy Huff?"

"No, kid was sixteen, I mean Frazer."

Rake nodded, and waved a hovering waiter away. He poured Deakin more wine.

"Frazer was hooked, pills, boys and money, and they were his good points," Deakin winked. "Ask around."

"I'm asking you, John. You've made the rehearsed speech, I want the meat, and what did you mean when you said the boy was a talent?"

"Come again?"

"You said he *was* a talent."

Deakin lit another cigarette from the stub of his first and shrugged.

"He died."

"When?"

"I don't know, I think I read it. I must have read it, or heard about it - somewhere. You know how it is, these kids are

12

highly strung, they swim about then the sharks come, they smell blood in the water. Parnes, Frazer, they corral these little urchins, zhoosh them up and turn them out, make a few quid and then they dump them. Not my scene is it? It's a racket, Christ Rake, you need to get down to Denmark Street, have a chat with the Yids, or the Two I's, like I say, not my scene. Not at all."

The big blonde fellow lurched over to the table and leant heavily upon it, craning his neck down to look at Deakin. His slab of a face was red at the cheeks and his deep-set blue eyes were swimming in his head. He sounded Norwegian or maybe Danish, though his English was fine.

"You fuck, fucker," he said. "Deakin, fuck, fucker," he said again for emphasis.

"Good evening, Viggo, Happy New Year," said Deakin.

"All right fucking cunt, Deakin. All right? Fuck you Deakin, my money."

"Viggo, this is Chief Inspector Rake, of the Metropolitan Police."

"I don't give a fig fuck for that, Deakin. My money, I give a fuck about that."

"You bring me to the nicest places, Rakey," Deakin said, smiling at Rake. Rake took another sip of wine; his eyes steady on Deakin, his right hand resting nonchalantly on the linen.

"Me money, fifty bull's-eye Deakin, fifty. I laid it fair and square, for the painting you promised me, said you had it. No painting."

The blonde looked at Rake, he bowed his head and tried to focus, and then he drew his finger across his nose, like he had an itch.

"I'm sorry my friend," he put out his hand as if to shake Rake's, then turned back to Deakin, and then turned to Rake again.

"He's your china plate, eh? Nothing for you to worry about, just this *rotte*. You keep your nose out of it and we got no problem, okay? See he said he had this painting by Sutherland, offered me, I paid up – no show, no painting."

Rake didn't respond, he kept his eyes on Deakin. Deakin kept his eyes fixed on Rake. The blonde proffered his hand again, more aggressively. "Okay, or what?" This time Rake took the hand in his.

"There, see? I got no trouble with you, policeman." He tried to retract his hand, but Rake held it, and applied pressure. An onlooker would have noticed nothing, nothing except that the blonde's face began to blossom and sweat greased his brow. He grunted. Rake remained impassive, looking at Deakin, who sniggered girlishly. Rake suddenly pulled the man's hand roughly towards him, and he looked into his eyes, steady and unflinching.

"Go back to your table and finish your meal," he pulled again and was nose to nose with the blonde. "And then leave." He let the hand go with a snap of his wrist and waved the blonde away. The man held his right hand in his left, cradling it like a wounded puppy. He shot a look at Deakin, who bent his pinkie in a strange salute, wagging it coquettishly.

"Ta ta Viggo, lovely bumping into you again, we must catch up properly."

"You lousy Lilly loving luder, see you soon, rovhul cunt. And fuck you copper cunt."

Viggo walked back to his table and sat, talking conspiratorially with his companions. They looked over at Deakin and Rake, but had seemingly decided to keep their counsel.

"So, John, continue."

"Oh, I've lost my thread. Anyway, I've got an appointment." Deakin stood, a little unsteadily. Rake pulled a pound note from his coat and slid it towards Deakin who was preoccupied, stealing a sideways glance at Viggo and his cronies.

"Sit down John."

"I've got to be offski."

Rake kicked Deakin's chair a foot from the table and cocked a finger like a pistol, pointing. Deakin sat back down and turned his chair away from Viggo.

"What about what you're not telling me, John?"

"Like what am I not telling you?"

14

"Like about your little holiday in Tangier last November." Deakin picked up his wine glass, his hand was shaking, but this didn't necessarily signify anything.

"It wasn't a holiday, I was working for Vogue, it was an assignment. Want to see the snaps?"

"Yes, very much, in fact I insist."

"I'll drop them round."

"Do that, soon. We can put some names to some faces. Was Frazer there?"

Deakin shrugged, there was a sudden eruption of noise from Viggo's table and Deakin tensed and his eyes swivelled in his head.

"Is that the time? I've got to be somewhere."

"I know Frazer was there, in Tangier, in November."

"He might have been, I was working at Barbara Hutton's soiree, and I was thrown out. I'm going, I really am." Deakin pushed the pound note back across the table and stood.

"I know Frazer was in Tangier, same time as you. Was he at the party?"

"I didn't see him."

"I want to see those photographs, pronto."

"All right, all right. Watch my back, okay?"

Rake nodded and watched as Deakin took a long walk around the periphery of the room. He exited without looking back and was taken by the night. The waiter approached and placed a bottle of Chianti on the table.

"From the party over there," he said, indicating Viggo's table. Rake looked over and Viggo raised his glass.

"Jubel!" he said.

"Take it back," said Rake to the waiter. He paid the bill, stood and walked past the clique to collect his coat and hat. As he passed the table Viggo looked up at him.

"Something wrong with the vintage?"

"I like to choose who I drink with, Viggo."

"You drink with that afskum, he's no good, that one. I'll catch up with him."

"Then I'll catch up with you." Rake patted Viggo on the shoulder and walked onto Dean Street. The sleet had stopped

15

falling, leaving the street slick and pulpy underfoot, the roadway coloured with a rainbow of oil under the neon. Rake headed toward The Colony Room and Muriel, and perhaps some warmth and even fellowship on this, the last night of the decade.

## Chapter Two

Deeming looked at his reflection then picked the heavy gilt mirror from the dark wall and took it to the window. He propped the mirror on the sill and stepped back. The winter sun was setting over the park creating a perfect slanting beam that laid bare the fact that his alopecia was worsening. He walked to the kitchen and cracked four eggs into a bowl and whisked them with a fork, and then he lathered his scalp in the mixture, wrapped a towel about his skull, dragged a second towel about his shoulders and sat at the table. He picked several strands of strong black hair from between his fingers and wiped them onto the towel. He spread his fingers, sticky with egg, webbed almost, and then he simply sat, forlorn and bitter, as the day gave way to evening, the room darkening around him. There was a New Years Eve party scheduled for ten somewhere in Shepherds Market, but before that Alfie was due to pick him up and take him to the Gargoyle for drinks with a few of the chaps. The telephone started to trill in the living room. Deeming stood and rinsed his hands at the kitchen sink, and went to the instrument, he waited, it was Danby.

"Hello, boss?"
Deeming grunted, the egg had started to run down his cheek making the muscle tic at the corner of his mouth.

"Alfie's not well, got the flu, so I'm driving you tonight."

"Why'd he tell you, what – am I an ogre or something, you seen him?"

"No, he rung me, anyway boss, I'll drive you, it's not a problem."

"No, I want you to find Deakin."

"I've been round to David Archer's gaff, no one's at home. I can get Billy on to it."

"No, you're on to it. Alfie is driving me."

There was a long silence; Deeming could picture Danby's face, mouthing a silent expletive at the receiver.

"Anything else?" he said.

"No, I'll let Alfie know. He won't be happy."

"He's only driving, he doesn't need to be elevated."

17

Deeming put the receiver back in its cradle and went into the bathroom. He showered and dried himself meticulously, using a new flannel to dry between his toes. Then he powdered his fleshy torso and patted Aqua Velva onto his cheeks, his neck and his wrists. He looked once again at his hair, combing it back across his head and patting it into place. Then he put on his dressing gown and went to lie on his bed, to await the arrival of his driver and the revelries to come.

At eight thirty the buzzer sounded. Deeming rose from the bed and picked up the entry phone that resided on the wall by his front door. A nasal voice squawked, followed by a coughing fit.
"It's me boss", it was Alfie Atkins in person.
"Wait in the motor. You feeling better?"
Without waiting for an answer, Deeming hung up and walked into his dressing room. He chose a double-breasted blue pinstripe, a royal blue on white shirt with a double cuff and his favourite brogues, in black, obviously. Deeming went about getting dressed in the way he undertook every action that required vigour, slowly, attending to detail. It was all about detail. He tied his Hermes with a full Windsor knot and pinned a small diamond solitaire stick through the silk. Finally he folded the matching silk handkerchief into his breast pocket and stepped back to admire his reflection. He attended once again to his hair, looking left, then right, finally collecting his shaving mirror and holding it to inspect the coiffure from widows peak to nape of neck. If he didn't sit under direct light he would be fine, he told himself. He walked into his bedroom and opened a narrow drawer, selecting a pair of Omega Prestige cufflinks in gold. Deeming checked every room, ensuring that the toilets were flushed, the kitchen appliances were turned off and that the lights were extinguished in each room. He took the lift and walked out of the rear door of the mansion block to where Alfie stood smoking, resting his buttocks against the Daimler. Deeming shot his cuffs and Alfie Atkins flicked the cigarette into darkness, took the cufflinks and threaded them carefully through the proffered buttonholes. Deeming squeezed the boy's cheek affectionately.

"Danby tells me you're a bit under the weather, son."
"Yeah, well, it's the flu isn't it."
Deeming climbed into the back of the Daimler and slid the partition window closed. He didn't want the germs, at least not until he knew it was a risk worth taking. Alfie shuffled into the drivers seat and turned the engine over. They cruised towards Meard Street and the Gargoyle. Alfie watched his boss in the rear-view mirror as streetlights washed the big man's face in orange and yellow bands of radiance. When Deeming caught his eye, Alfie concentrated on the road, shifting his weight in the seat and focusing. Deeming made him nervous. He made everyone nervous. It was the suspense, the sense that any displeasure could flare into a volatile, untameable eruption that might be meted out summarily or might simmer, to be expelled in the deep of the night, in the silken chamber of his bedroom.

The Daimler pulled up on Dean Street at its junction with Meard Street. Deeming told Alfie to go and park the car, then meet him upstairs, but by the time the boy got back, Deeming was standing on the street.
"What's up boss?"
"It's horrible, like Miss Havisham's wedding cake, I remember when it was a nice place, but it's like everything else nowadays, miserable. Where's the motor?"
"Romilly Street."
"We'll have a stroll then, eh? Stop off at the Coach, get you a medicinal brandy, then you can take me home."
"What about the party?"
"You're poorly, son, can't be out and about on a night like this, got to take care of you. Tell you what; I'll rustle you up a nice omelette, eh? What about a hot toddy take the chill off? Lovely, watch a bit of telly get an early night. You look peaky, need some Vicks rubbing on that chest."
"Shit way to spend New Years Eve though, ain't it?"
"You being snippy, Alfie, eh? I'm doing you a favour, boy, I'm being what's it called?"
"I don't know, what is it called boss?"

"You little twerp," Deeming said. His voice had that edge and Alfie Atkins knew he'd pushed it that bit too far. Deeming walked down Dean Street and the boy followed, head bowed, a supplicant now, seeing the whole dreadful evening laid out before him and helpless to alter its course. He'd been counting on the party, on Deeming getting blotto and falling asleep, as was his wont. But he'd been scuppered, his hopes gone to nought. Typical, thought Alfie Atkins as he skipped along the wet street, catching up to Deeming, working through how to rescue the night, how to rescue himself and escape the man's florid excesses.

The telephone started ringing at two thirty in the morning. Rake woke with a start on the third ring. He'd been dreaming, something about Ruth. When he reached over and picked the receiver from its cradle he was surprised to hear her voice coming down the line. She sounded tipsy and he could hear the sound of merry voices and music in the background.

"Cyril, Cyril?"
"Hello sweetheart, Happy New Year, you all right?"
"I'm fine darling, Happy New Year, where are you?"
"Love, you 'phoned *me*, I'm at the flat, where are you?"
"I'm at home darling".

Rake thought of their house in Putney, and his heart flipped over. He was hung over, properly now, a bastard head and a sandpaper tongue stranded in his dry mouth.

"Darling?" she repeated.
"Sorry, I drifted, I was asleep. Can I go and get some water? Will you hang on?"

A man's voice echoed in Rake's ear, an American twang, though he couldn't quite make out the words.

"No, don't worry Cyril, we're going on. I just, I just wanted you to know I'm thinking of you. Sending love, darling, take care…"
"Ruth, are you driving?"
"No, no, don't worry, darling."

The American came through, louder now and clearer.

20

"Baby, you coming or what? Who you talkin' to? Hey, move it or lose it honey, I'm going." Ruth had obviously put her hand over the receiver and Rake overheard some muffled interchange that he really could have done without. Then Ruth came back on.

"I've got to go, take care Cyril, I hope nineteen sixty is a good year for you, I really do, I do, I do."

The line crackled and then there was just the hum humming and humming in his head. He sat for a while, as if hoping for some species of change that might come, like a Christmas miracle, some change in his circumstance. He placed the receiver back down and was reaching for a cigarette when the doorbell rang. Rake stood and walked to the window. He looked down onto the Charing Cross Road, at the slovenly thoroughfare, ill lit and hostile seeming in that moment. He lifted the sash and leaned out, calling. A figure scurried from the alleyway and looked up.

"Let me in", the figure bawled. It was Deakin.

Alfie Atkins limped from the apartment block at three in the morning of January first nineteen sixty. His hip was bruised, his buttocks welted and his ribs sore, but not fractured, he thought. As usual, there were no marks that might be visible to his mum, which he supposed was a blessing. His mum, Joan, thought Mister Deeming was a saint, a benefactor, "If it weren't for that man you'd be doin' a stretch, mark my words, Alfie," she would say. "You'd be sharing porridge with your father, boy." Alfie's father was serving time in the Scrubs on a receiving charge. His girl Sophie had the measure of Deeming, but was ignorant of the shaming fact of the relationship. She just thought he was snide, which, of course, he was. Alfie climbed into the Daimler and headed east towards home. There was no traffic to speak of, and he got to Ilford well before dawn, parking in the lock up paid for by Deeming, and walking the twenty minutes it took to get to Belmont Road and the upstairs flat, also paid for by Deeming. He fried some bacon and folded it into a slab of bread, washing it down with a mug of tea, and then he went gratefully to his bed. He tried to masturbate, thinking of Sophie, but it was no good. So he shut his eyes and attempted to sleep. Finally, as dawn broke, chill and forbidding, Alfie Atkins let it all go and drifted away, to somewhere better.

Rake and Deakin sat in the policeman's room going over the photographs that the little man had pulled from his coat, along with a bottle of Cherry Brandy that he'd liberated from David Archers flat. The photos were taken at Barbara Hutton's stone palace in the heart of the Kasbah in Tangier. These pictures, snapped, Deakin claimed, for an assignment orchestrated by Vogue, portrayed the excesses of an evening spent amongst belly dancers, the blue men of Morocco, snake charmers and the various and varied celebrities and spivs who had attended the soiree.

"She called me the second nastiest man she'd ever met and had me escorted from the premises," said Deakin. "Cheeky cow, I mean, the place was full of lepers, not literally, of course, but figuratively. It was all a bit Sodom and the other one."

Rake perused the images, he recognised a number of people, famous faces, but not Logan Frazer.

"You look disappointed Rakey, not what you're after? "

"No, not what I'm after, John. Is this it?"

"That's all, chum, sorry."

Rake took a pull from the bottle and grimaced as the thick, sickly sweet liquor curdled in his stomach. He looked over at the alarm clock sitting on the suitcases he used as a bedside cabinet. It was nearly five; he needed to be up by eight. He was going in for nine thirty, the bank holiday notwithstanding.

"You'd better be off, I need to catch some shut eye."

Deakin scratched his chin and then he pushed the cork back into the bottle and leaned back on the sofa.

"Thing is, Rakey, I've rather burned my bridges at David's. He's back in town today, and he's likely to notice the book issue, and some other trifles. I need to keep my head down, at least until he's blown off some steam. I thought, I *hoped*, you'd let me doss down here, just for a couple of days. I might be able to give some proper attention to details, you know, about Morocco; I'm thinking there were other faces around. I could ask about, I'm

22

sure I could come up with some useful stuff. I could nip into Vogue, have a go at the contact sheets, what do you think?"

Rake stood up and stretched the kinks out of his back. He looked down at Deakin, who had somehow spread his small frame, as if he was rooting himself to the sofa.

"If only you'd bought Scotch, John."

"He's hidden all the decent stuff, Rakey. Honestly, I can't go back to Archer's until he's calmed himself down." He spread his aubergine lips across his chin in an approximation of a smile. He looked grotesque, mashing it up like a little tart. Rake went over to his bed and dragged off the ratty top blanket, flinging it over to Deakin.

"You need to be quiet, I've really got to sleep, you'll have to be on your way when I leave."

"Quiet as a church mouse, honestly, quiet as the grave." Rake left the flat and walked along the hall to the lavatory. As he shat he swore an oath, knowing that it wasn't good. He pulled up his clothing and looked into the bowl. It was as if someone had thrown half a glass of Rioja onto the porcelain. He pulled the chain and fastened his trousers. Then he scrubbed the pan with the hideous brush and washed his hands in the mean little corner sink, thinking that he really must get to a doctor, realising he probably wouldn't he went back to his room. Deakin was snuggled under the blanket, his coat rolled and folded into a makeshift pillow. Rake turned off the light and got undressed, illuminated only by the street lamp. Then he climbed into his bed and closed his eyes. He was aware of Deakin's breathing, and of the rattle that caught on the little man's outward breath. He dreamed that Deakin was standing over him, naked, touching himself. At least, he thought it was a dream, hoped it was anyway.

# Chapter Three

Rake woke to the alarm, it was eight am and he looked over at the undraped window and saw that it was raining heavily. He propped himself on an elbow and saw Deakin sitting up with a cigarette dangling from his lips. The man's eyes looked strangely intent, as if he'd been studying Rake whilst he'd been sleeping. Deakin pulled the blanket away and climbed from the sofa. He was naked below the waist, looking, Rake thought, like a plucked Turkey, with the giblets set askew.

"Porridge?" Deakin wheezed.

"Put some clothes on."

Deakin sat down on the blanket and pulled on his skivvies. Rake thought, *that blanket is heading for the bins, as soon as*. Deakin walked through to the kitchenette and started banging through cupboards.

"Salt? Where's the bloody salt? Christ man, there's nothing here."

"I eat in the canteen, just put the kettle on. Make the tea while I sort myself out. You'll have to leave before me, I've got a car picking me up." Rake got out of bed and began to dress. Deakin wandered in and leaned against the doorframe.

"Ashamed to be seen with me, eh?"

"Damned right. You're a source and a possible person of interest, and a fucking nuisance."

"Oh, nice."

"Piss off John, I'm not in the mood."

"I'll go now then, shall I?"

"Yes please," said Rake abstractedly, searching for his socks.

Deakin leavened himself from the frame and walked over to the sofa, picking through his clothes and pulling on his jersey.

"I had thought of something, but maybe I just wont bother," he peeved.

"I can't be doing this."

"There were people at the hotel that night, the Continental. I think Frazer was one of them. They were supposed to go to the do, but they didn't. I seem to remember they included Frazer, and that boy, Huff, and someone else, who I think you might know, actually."

Rake looked over at the man, who was standing, half undressed still, rolling a cigarette. Rake gestured irritably. Deakin continued to roll the cigarette, running his dreadful tongue along the edge of the paper. Rake knew the game, but despite himself he capitulated.

"And who might that have been John?"

"I don't honestly know, Nigel something, or Neil. But he was a face, reeked of the underworld, a right nasty piece of work", said the little man from within a cloud of blue smoke. "I think I might have taken a roll of film, at the hotel, you know how it is when you've made a night of it. It sort of drifts back in snatches, like dreams."

Noel Deeming lay, quite still in his capacious bed, listening to the bells of Christ Church bringing him the day on a cascading knell of optimism, joy and celebration that struck him as nothing short of sarcastic. He looked over to where Danby sat, half in shadow, on the Regency Chaise Longue.

"Go and shoot those fucking bell ringing cunts," Deeming said.

"Campanologists."

"Go and shoot those fucking campanologist cunts."

"Want a cup of tea?"

"What's the weather doing?"

"Raining, tea?"

"Deakin?"

"No, he's gone to ground."

"Don't fanny about, Danby. Put it on top of your list."

Deeming sat up, lifted his heavy legs from the bed and shuffled his feet into slippers. He turned on the bedside lamp and pulled the sheets back to inspect the mattress, no shit, no blood, so he flung the bedding back haphazardly.

"Is the girl in?"

"It's New Years Day."

"I'll make the brew, I don't want any of your invalid tea. Where's Alfie?"

"On his way in, won't be long."

"We're lunching at Rules, one thirty, just me, you and Bender."

"What Bender?"

"H. H., the others don't count for cock. Only H. H. doesn't know he's coming - yet, so you and Alfie go and bring him. Make sure he is properly dressed; little berk hasn't got a clue. No deportment that lot south of the river, still drinking their tea out of fucking saucers. You can drop me first, I'll have a drink upstairs, but take him straight to the table then you come and join me, leave the cunt to stew for half an hour, let him get drinking, loosen him up a bit."

"What if he's reluctant?"

Deeming pulled on his dressing gown and headed for the bedroom door.

"Clarify the situation for him," he said.

Alfie Atkins climbed into the Daimler and headed towards Mayfair. He shifted in the seat to get his arse comfortable, grimacing at the memory of Deeming and wincing at the thought of the night ahead, of all the nights to come. He was saving desperately to build a future for him and Sophie, but it was at a cost that was hard to reconcile. He drove through Barking, Sophie lived on Ripple Road, and he thought about popping in to wish her a Happy New Year, but she was aggy about his not being there for last nights big shindig, and she'd probably still be asleep anyway, so he pressed on towards the city.

Danby stood looking down at the car park when Alfie pulled up. He let the curtain drop and mashed his cigarette into the big green onyx ashtray that sat on the wine table.

"Car's here, boss," he said.

"Go down and tell him where and what. I'll be five minutes."

Danby shrugged into his Aquascutum Camel hair overcoat and walked down the back staircase and out onto the car park. By the time he reached the motor his long greying hair was plastered across his head and the coat was drenched. He climbed into the Daimler and sat alongside Alfie.

"Don't worry Alfie boy, we'll come to you."
"Whatever."
"You want to watch that."
"Sorry."
"When his Lordship comes down just pull up to the doorway. He's not in a good mood so watch the mardy palaver and straighten yourself out. Rough night?" Nothing from the boy, "I told him you were poorly, but he wanted you and only you, what could I do?"

Again Alfie said nothing. They sat and watched the rain, Danby keeping a weather eye on the doorway.

"We're dropping him off at Rules, Maiden Lane. Then we need to have a jaunt over the river to Catford to pick up one of the Bender's and take him back to the restaurant. Then the afternoon's yours, you might nip to Barking and visit that little palony you've got stashed. Get your whistle wet for half an hour, or however long it takes you children."

Alfie shot the big man a look, but kept his counsel. Danby was always riding him about Sophie. He'd have to let it go, have to swallow it, though it was hard to digest. They sat in silence, the rain whipping icily onto the windscreen carried on blasts of wind that roared horizontally between the tall buildings.

"He's here," said Danby. Alfie started the car and they pulled up at the entrance. Deeming climbed in the back. He leaned over and squeezed Alfie's shoulder.

"Happy New Year, Alfie boy. You all right?"
"Good as gold, boss."
"Maiden Lane, you got the gist?"
Alfie Atkins nodded, reversed and headed through the canyon of buildings and past Mount Street Gardens heading towards the restaurant to decant Mister Deeming.

Forty minutes later the Daimler was speeding over London Bridge heading south. Alfie and Danby got to Fordel Road and slowed, looking for number eleven. They pulled up outside a bay windowed terrace, dour and peeling in the muted light of that frowning morning.

"Want me to come with you?" Alfie said.

"No, son – just go and swing the motor round and keep the engine running," Danby said. " Won't be a tick". He reached under the seat and pulled out a short piece of lead pipe, bound at one end in thick tape, and slipped it up his sleeve.

"Be prepared, eh?" He exited the car and walked up the path. He took a look through the window and tapped on the glass, beckoning. The front door opened ajar and Danby spoke into the darkness beyond, then he placed his palm against the frosted glass and was gone. Alfie drove along Fordel Road and reversed into a driveway, turning expertly to return to number eleven facing towards St Fillans Road and ways west. As he pulled up the door opened and a very thin and shabby man exited the house, followed by Danby. This was H.H. Bender in his pomp; Alfie noted that H.H.'s pyjama trousers flapped beneath his suit, soaking up puddled water like a dirty sponge. His shoes were unlaced and he was struggling into his Macintosh. The dishevelled Mister Bender was bundled into the back of the car and Danby pressed in beside him. A gaggle of men and a woman left the house and stood hesitantly on the path, talking excitedly at one another, then one fellow stepped forward heading purposely for the gate.

"Hi Ho Silver, Mister Atkins, quick as you like," said Danby. Alfie slipped the car into gear and eased the big machine smoothly away from the kerb.

Rake walked along the first floor corridor of West End Central police station followed by Detective Sergeant Peter Sweet, who had driven him from the flat. Both men were feeling fragile, Sweet having attended the previous evenings ball at Hainault, along with many of his colleagues and their wives. The two had conducted a peevish exchange in the car and Sweet peeled off to talk with a uniformed officer, leaving Rake to head into his office alone. He flung his coat onto the rack then spun his hat in the same direction. It missed and flopped onto the floor by a wastepaper basket. Grunting, Rake bent to retrieve the hat and placed it on the hook with a disdainful look, as if his throw had been witnessed and it was the fault of the wayward trilby. He sat and picked up the receiver and tapped the intercom switch.

"Henrietta? Yes, and to you, love. Look sweetheart, I want you to track down the picture editor at Vogue. Right, yes you'll have to get him at home I would think, but there'll be someone at the office I'm guessing. As soon as you like, okay? Thanks." He hung up, and then picked up the receiver once again. "Before you do anything bring me a coffee, black and hot," he almost said *like you,* but refrained.

Sweet entered without knocking. He laid a sheaf of paper on the desk and turned to leave.

"Oh don't be a cunt Peter, sit down. What's this?"

"That list of Frazer's stable of acts."

"Sit! Right, off you go."

Sweet pulled out the chair and sat down as Rake leaned back and put his boots on the desk. He closed his eyes.

"I've got the names and the nom de plumes…"

"A nom de plume is a literary alias Peter; you're referring to a stage name." There followed a weighty silence, Rake opened an eye, then signalled for Sweet to get on with it, which he did.

"Well there's Rocky Saint James, he's in the charts at the moment with that song, 'From the Corner of my Eye', real name is Patrick Gupta."

"You're pulling my leg."

"He's Anglo Indian. Then you've got Chuck Blizzard; real name Charles Goole, then there's Johnny Rocket."

"Oh for fuck's sake."

"Real name Phillip Fry, he's a leather boy, you know, leather trousers, leather jacket, leather gloves with rings and a cycle chain for a belt."

"You a fan?"

"No, but Christine likes him."

"You want to take her in hand son, really."

The door opened and Henrietta waltzed in carrying a coffee and a plate of biscuits. She laid them on the desk along with a slip of paper.

"That number you wanted, sir."

"You ever heard of Johnny Rocket?"

"Yes, but I don't like pop music, sir."

"Very sound, thanks sweetheart."

They waited as Henrietta left the office. Rake was aware that Sweet was watching him watching her, his eyebrows dancing.

"Well what of it?"

"Nothing," said Sweet. "Been a bit of gossip, that's all."

"She's bloody lovely, but she's married."

"She's half a nignog."

"I've got eyes, and you can cut that crap out right now Sergeant, I mean it."

"All right, sorry boss."

"Look just fuck off, get that list typed and copied and find out who's nearest, we'll pay them a visit."

"Right you are, and sorry if I caused any offense, I didn't mean to."

"Crack on and shut up. Address, car - and let the reserve room know where we're going. Ten minutes, all right?"

It was nearer eleven when the two policemen drove west towards the Shepherds Bush end of Holland Road. Rake was mystified and steaming; the phone call to Michael Daniels, the picture editor at Vogue had revealed the fact that Deakin had last worked for the magazine in 1954 when he'd been sacked, apparently for a second time. Any photographs of the Hutton party were taken before he'd been canned. So what had he been doing in Tangier in November of last year and why was he lying? He shook it off until later, lit a Craven A and spoke to Sweet.

"Tell me about this fellow we're going to delight with our company."

"Stage name is Elmo Tweak, real name Kenneth Muir, he's more of a Variety act, a comic, song and dance man with a bit of saucy patter thrown in, like a tatty Max Miller. But he had a hit with 'Be my Fairy Angel on the Christmas Tree' a couple of years back and Frazer took him on. He's faded since, but he's still active on the circuit."

"'Be my Fairy Angel on the Christmas Tree and I'll be your little Snowman on the Cake.' Jesus, Ruth bought it, played it all through that Christmas, drove me mad, I spun it out of the window on Boxing Day along with her new cardy, a present from her mother, horrible thing with plastic buttons and pink flowers. Ken Muir, I know the name."

"You felt his collar a while back, soliciting. He told the Magistrate it was entrapment and the beak swallowed it."

"You rehearsed that."

They pulled up at a big house, once a nice villa but frowsy now and split into flats. They climbed out of the Wolsey and ascended steps that led to a flaking door. Sweet rang the bell and they waited. It was perishing and Rake's teeth started to chatter. He felt sick, tired and extremely jaded; he thumped his fist onto the woodwork. They waited some more, then Rake put his brogues to work, toe punting the door energetically a couple of times. Finally they heard slippers shuffling along the hallway and the door opened to reveal a woman, tabarded, with hair pulled up under a stained floral scarf.

"What you want, banging like that, I mean?"

"Police missus, we're here to see Kenneth Muir, he in?" Sweet offered.

"Well what you mean kicking the door? Which one kicked the door? Was it you? I was upstairs, I can't run up and down stairs, not with my rheumatis, what were you thinking?"

"Sorry Ma," Rake said. "We just want a word with Mister Muir. Now, is he in?"

"He won't be up yet, he was performing last night. He's an artiste you know, famous he is, got a lot of them here, artistes I mean. He's Elmo Tweak."

"Tell you what, sweetheart," this was Rake again, edging past her into the vestibule. " You go and put the kettle on and we'll give him a gentle knock up, alright?"

"Oh I say, bit pushy."

"A nice brew, eh love? Only way to start the day, upstairs is it?"

"Well, yes – number five, on the second floor."

"We'll find it, don't worry, he'll be right as rain once he's got that lovely cup of tea, warm the pot, I'm gasping."

"Warm the pot, warm the pot? I'll give you warm the pot, bloomin' cheek! Warm your own ruddy pot, I'm not a skivvy."

They went quickly along the worn carpet and onto the stairs, finding number five at the end of a dark landing. Rake knocked.

"Mister Muir, this is Detective Chief Inspector Rake from West End Central. We need a quick word."

There came the sound of movement from within - bedsprings squeaking, a groan, an oath. Rake knocked again and repeated his soliloquy. Eventually the door opened ajar and a familiar face, or at least the right half of it peeked out blinking into the shadows. A high effeminate voice carried on a waft of stale alcohol and burnt gravy greeted them.

"What do you want?"

"We want a word, Mister Muir, or is it Tweak? Won't take long, five minutes."

"What's it about? I mean I'm not dressed."

"Just five minutes, honest."

Muir pulled the door open and shuffled back a foot or two. As soon as he saw the man Rake realised he knew the face, from the pinch – what, five years previous? Maybe longer, he thought, and from the television. He was scrawny, pale as alabaster, his head ringed by a halo of thinning hennaed curls. He was wearing an outsized kimono and was likely naked beneath, his long legs visible as he crossed them, sitting uncomfortably upright on the sagging bed. He looked to Rake like a Bacon painting, hemmed in and breathless, a man in aspic. There was only one chair, and neither policeman chose to utilise it. They towered over Muir, all three feeling the strain.

"Well, go on then, what's this all about?"

"Logan Frazer," Rake said, as Sweet flipped open his pocket notebook and stood poised.

"All right if D.C. Sweet takes a few notes?" Rake continued. Muir shrugged and pulled the kimono over his knees in a strangely demure gesture.

"You're aware that Frazer is deceased, well I'm afraid that, contrary to reports that he died in a fire, he was in point of fact murdered." Rake watched Muir closely, checking the reaction. Muir was unreadable; Rake thought that perhaps he was under the influence of narcotics. Then he realised that the man had had a facelift, probably performed by a Smithfield bummaree.

"I'm sorry to be the bearer of sad tidings."

"I'm not surprised, do I look surprised? Well, I'm not frankly, so there, I'm not going to say much because I haven't got much to say, my mother said to me, she said that if you haven't got a kind word better to say nothing, so I won't. But, if I *did* have something to say, it wouldn't be kind, not at all, it really wouldn't, so," his voiced trailed into silence.

The policemen stood, still and quiet. Rake had taught Sweet about silence, nature abhors a vacuum he had said, and it was true, hold the silence and the untrained voice will eventually be heard, and soon enough it came.

"Anyway," said Muir. "Got a fag?"

Rake proffered a cigarette and then a lighter, and Muir inhaled gratefully, following up with a hacking, phlegmy cough.

"Ta."

"So Frazer, you're not surprised then?"

"Do I look surprised? Don't think so, look Logan was a tight arsed Scottish bastard like that other Yid Parnes. Got us all on wages, stitched me right up, I mean it's all very well for the yobbo's, they're kids really, but it's my career, ending up like this, well I mean. I've got to troll up to bloody Yarmouth tomorrow, then Cromer, and – where else?" He thought for a moment, biting a nail. "Southend, Clacton – oh, it's a game, and the tat I have to work with! Well, you've no idea, it's heartrending, but what's a boy to do?"

"And Frazer?"

"Oh, yes – sorry, Frazer, well I'm not surprised. How did it happen?"

"He was beaten to death."

"Oh nasty," Muir became thoughtful. "No really, alright that is really tawdry, and then they set the place on fire? Yes well, not nice, eh? Any idea who might have, no – you wouldn't be here, I suppose."

"It happened just after a holiday in Tangier, were you part of the expedition?"

"Me, no no, I'm not part of the dans la foule, ducky, know what I mean? Oh no, I wasn't invited. It was all very hush hush, only those in the know."

"So who was in the know?"

"Was I there? If I wasn't there I don't care, that's my motto."

"But surely there must have been gossip, amongst you all, a bit of banter, about the holiday. You strike me as someone with his ear to the ground, and you don't want to be seen as withholding now, do you? It's murder, after all. We could, reluctantly, have to take you in for questioning, better just deal with it here and now, save all the fuss, and any unfortunate publicity." Rake turned the chair around and perched, lighting his own cigarette and letting the atmosphere take on some weight. Muir stubbed out his cigarette huffily and fidgeted his bottom on the bed.

"I don't know much, so don't quote me," he said looking pointedly at Sweet. "Frazer went, and Maurice – to look after Roy Huff, didn't do a good job there, did he?"

"What do you mean?"

"What do I mean – where you been, love? Roy topped hisself out there in the Kasbah, didn't he? Slit his wrists, right there in the room he shared with Maurice, you know, big old Deacon Blood, couldn't look after Goldfish - they put him in charge of Little Mickey Magnet, asking for trouble."

"Why asking for trouble?"

"You ever seen pictures of Roy, or seen him on the box? Oh dolly filiome, lovely looking boy, and sweet, very nice boy, but my God, wild? I mean, he was a wild child, but lovely, no he was, lovely lad, shame, I was crushed I was, *crushed*."

"Why was John Deakin there?"

"That worm? He was there with some big homie, don't know his name, just some geezer with loads of dinarly apparently, do you know Deakin? Can't abide the man myself, so anyway, he was there with this fella. That's all I know, oh, and Larry Parnes turned up too. They was all going to the Hutton place for a party. I wasn't on the list, Cinderella Tweak here got left in the scullery, shame eh?"

"Anyone else there?"

"How am I supposed to know? I only know about Roy 'cos he, you know – as I said, and Deakin 'cos Maurice told me at the funeral, Roy's I mean, I didn't go to Frazer's, too many…" he made a hooking gesture with his forefinger over his nose.

As they descended the long dark staircase Sweet grimaced and shook his head.

"What?" Rake asked, knowing.

"Can't stand 'em."

"Who?"

"That sort, degenerate perverts."

Rake stopped at the foot of the stairs and looked up at Sweet, halting him with a gimlet eye.

"Maybe you need to request a transfer, son. Head off to Suffolk or something, or go into Vice where you can spend your time rounding them up and giving them some stick. This is the work, Peter. The work!"

"Well what do you think?"

"I think about solving this killing, and I think about the work, and if you need smelling salts every time you meet someone who is different from you and Christine and your pals at the golf club you can fuck off, because I don't need that kind of help, alright?"

They walked together into the stinging rain, two drab policemen, each with faces tingling with the bitter cold and the bitter realisation of a friendship beginning to fracture and fail.

# Chapter Four

Noel Deeming sat at a discreet table at Rules, sipping a glass of Ludon de Geman 1928. Sandwiched uncomfortably between him and Danby, H. H. Bender bristled with constrained vexation.

"Have an Oyster H., try the Maldon Rock, fucking lovely son," he picked up a shell and waved it under Bender's nose. "Smell that, just like the sea. They say swallow them whole, but I always take two good chews, bit of lemon drop of Tabasco – ambrosial, go on."

"I don't eat seafood, it's treif . It's against my faith."

"Fuck me H., larks you lot get up to, you're already damned."

Deeming squeezed a muslin covered half lemon over the Oyster along with a heavy dash of hot sauce. He stuck his finger into the melange and lifted the meat so it rested unconstrained on the shell before proffering the mollusc once again to Bender.

"Try it, just one, don't know what you're missing," Danby said.

"You ain't eaten none," Bender huffed.

"Keeping room for my Venison."

"Fuckin' eat it you cunt," said Deeming. "I prepared it myself, I prepared it with my own hands, it's a perfect fucking specimen."

Deeming moved the shell to his left hand, and with his right he took hold of Bender's nose and jerked upwards. Then he clattered the shell into the man's teeth, lifted it and tipped the Oyster into his mouth

"Suck you nasty little pig, or you'll be swallowing the shell."

Bender slurped the meat into his mouth and gulped it down. Choking he grasped his wine glass and polished it off, as if taking in an enormous pill.

"There, what about it, lovely eh?" Deeming said, dipping his hand into his finger bowl and wiping it on a serviette.

"He looks like he enjoyed it," Danby said. "He looks well satisfied."

Bender shook his head and shivered. Danby refilled the man's glass and buttered a crust of bread.

"Thought you were saving room for your Venison," Bender said peevishly. The party at the adjacent table were staring, but they returned to their meals when Danby gave them one of his looks.

"I heard a whisper H.," Deeming said. "What I heard was that you got hold of some photographs what you purchased from John Deakin recently when you was drinking at the Caves. Associate of mine was having a tipple there one lunchtime, there amongst the dropouts, and you was there with one of your little hooligans and Deakin sold you some pictures. Apparently my name was mentioned, it sort of wafted around in the ambience, but it struck my associate as funny, what with Deakin being a nasty little twerp and you being a cunt, that my name was in the ether at all," Deeming was looking right into Bender's shrunken little face. "Thought it was funny. Now, he thought it was funny H., but I don't see. I think it's a fucking liberty."

Bender opened his mouth to speak, but Danby put his hand on the man's knee and squeezed. Bender gasped and reddened, his eyes widening so they resembled nought so much as poached eggs swimming in a sea of ketchup. Deeming continued.

"Then I get this phone call, voice all muffled and distant, like some silly bollocks has got a hanky draped over the mouthpiece, like he's seen in that film," he clicked his fingers trying to recall the title. He looked to both men, but was met with blankness, so he continued. "He threatens me, I *know*, can you credit it? Can you fucking credit it? Can you, H? There am I, sat at home minding my own business, watching my new telly, glass of Cognac on the go, ready for a nice quiet evening enjoying Rawhide, when I start getting anonymous telephone calls, honestly H., I was perplexed, I was bewildered, I was nonplussed to say the least. Then I started to get wound up, this berk is saying that if I don't pop two grand in an envelope and drop it off at a specified location the photographs will be sent forthwith to the Daily Herald for publication. Now these pictures in and of themselves are neither here nor there H., but, and here's the rub,

*I am not someone who likes being treated like a cunt!* So I put two and two together and thought, I know what, I'll have a conflab with my old pal H. and set things straight. No need for fuss or bother, old H. will just hand over the snaps and tell me where I can find Deakin, then that'll be that – nice and tidy, all forgiven and forgotten. So, here we are, lovely bit of scran, smashing. Anyway H., drink up you cunt, enjoy your pud and then you can shoot off with Mister Danby and get the matter sorted."

Deeming sat back and took in the room. It was a beautiful space, antlers, plush velvet seating, white linen – proper, he thought, and proper historical – the oldest restaurant in the capital, class – and he absolutely loved it. Then he looked back at H. Bender, and his dander began to rise. New Years Day, favourite restaurant, a lovely evening ahead with Alfie, Danby here looking very smooth, then this, this *specimen* moaning about the lunch, quaffing the vin rouge like it was a pint of Watneys, sweaty cunt. Running round mouthing off, taking the mick, taking the proverbial, what nerve, what neck, little scrote.

"You little scrote!" Deeming suddenly exploded. Faces turned, conversation halted and a buzzing reverberated in his head. "I'm waiting. You lost your tongue? Because, I tell you what, you'd better find it cunt, or I'll cut it out with this, right here – right now." He had picked the steak knife from the tablecloth and was brandishing it with feeling.

"It's alright boss," Danby soothed. "It's in hand, leave it with me, that's right H., eh?"

The waiter arrived carrying Deeming's fillet of beef, Danby's Venison and Bender's Steak and Kidney Pudding and laid them as ordered on the table. Bender sat, still as a piece of taxidermy, looking at his dish. Deeming sliced his knife through the suet, revealing pieces of beef, kidney and gravy.

"Get stuck in – go on."

"I don't eat offal."

"Why'd you order it then?"

"I didn't," Bender said quietly, "you ordered it."

Deeming flicked his knife around the platter, pushing pieces of kidney to the side of the plate, making an unholy mess amongst the steaming suet.

"There you go, H., now be a good boy and eat up. I can't stand to watch a grown man chew the cud. Reminds me of my sister when we was nippers, Sunday lunch, chewing the fucking cud and retching, and there's me couldn't have my glass of pop till she'd finished. Mind you, mother was a lousy cook, couldn't boil an egg."

Deeming settled in to eating, it was suddenly as if he was alone in the room. The energy, once expended, seemed simply to have evaporated. Danby too began to enjoy his Venison. Bender took up his cutlery and picked warily at his meal, this tough little hood was now completely deflated, outmatched and outflanked. They ate in silence, Deeming taking his time, savouring each and every mouthful. When he's finished he laid his knife and fork carefully on his plate and spoke, almost politely.

"Sweet – no? Right then H., you and Mister Danby can get in a taxi and head back to wherever you've stashed the photographs. I assume you don't have the negatives? No, well, that'll be on Deakin then, eh? Right, you can pop off."

Danby stood and ushered Bender awkwardly into the aisle and helped him on with his coat, patting him on his shoulders with both hands and steering him along to the front of the restaurant. Deeming ordered a rhubarb crumble and a Cognac, lit his Davidoff cigar and sat back expansively, satisfied and relaxed, having got a result without compromising himself with unnecessary violence. He'd organise the reprisals later, once he'd collected the photos, the negatives, and John Deakin. Alfie Atkins walked to the table and stood, waiting to be acknowledged.

Rake knew something was wrong as soon as he opened the door to his flat. He'd stopped off at the Coach and Horses on his way home, ordered a Whisky Mac and asked about the sandwiches. He'd been offered a choice.

"Cheese and pickle or egg salad." Norman Balon had proffered, looking into the clear plastic display case. Rake had opted for the cheese. The bread was curling, as hard as cardboard, so after one bite he pushed the plate away and ordered another whisky. He took a look around the bar which was thinly spread with solitary drinkers, each bound in an intimate web of gloom and despondency, their eyes turned inward in sour contemplation. These were the forsaken ones, men without families, men alone, to whom this festive season was more of an insult than a celebration. Rake looked down at his drink, flushing with recognition and empathy. He drank the liquor down in one.

"I'll be off Norman, you take care."

"Did you catch up with Deakin?"

One of the punters, a small chap wearing a battered fedora and a rumpled Macintosh whom Rake didn't recognise piped up with a request for a pint of mild and bitter. Norman rounded on him.

"Piss off you rude cunt, I'm talking," he turned back to Rake. "I saw him nipping into David Archer's flat, looking very suspicious."

"What time was that?"

"About eleven this morning. Up to mischief if you ask me, little shit."

"Well, I've seen him, but thanks," an afterthought. " Anyone else been asking after him?"

"Funny that, but yes. Some big goon was asking about him, must have been yesterday, or the day before. Day before I think."

"Recognise him?"

"Vaguely, don't know his name. Bit of a face, big lunk, I told him to buy a drink or fuck off, I'm not an information bureau, I said."

"What did he look like?"

"Big, I mean tall, maybe six two or three. Thin, with a spivvy moustache, Camel hair coat, long grey hair under his hat. I sent him packing."

Rake wandered into the pitch of another wet night and walked back to the Charing Cross Road, ruminating on whether or not to telephone Ruth. As he opened his door the smell and the smoke assailed him. He could hear the sizzling of a hot pan and the clattering of activity in the kitchenette. He rounded the alcove to behold Deakin frying food, the radio on the Light Programme blaring "Lonely Boy" like a smack to the head,

40

Deakin twitching and gyrating to the music like an obscene automaton, singing into the spatula as if it were a microphone. Rake switched the radio off, Deakin turned startled, then a smile spread across his thin face.

"Alright Mister Rake? Got you a smashing dinner on the go. Got eggs, bacon, black pudding and sausages. I'll dish up and bung some bread into the pan, soak up the lovely juices."

"How the hell did you get in?"

"There was a spare key in that mug with the handle off. Thought I'd repay your kindness and deliver up a nice meal. Knew you wouldn't mind. I bet the canteen was shut today, wasn't it? 'Course it was, you eaten? 'Course you haven't, well you settle in, pour the whiskey, over there – over there, go on make yourself at home."

"I am at home. Where did all this come from, don't tell me, Archer's place. He'll *kill* you Deakin."

"Possession is eleven points of the law, and there are but twelve, you should know that! Anyway, he won't mind, redistribution of wealth, he loves all that."

Deakin dished up the supper, turned the flame up high and scraped the fatty remnants about in the pan. He dropped some slices of bread into the mess and pushed them around with a nicotine finger. Rake sat at the tiny Formica table and cut into a blackened sausage. It tasted lovely.

"I even bought condiments."

"Thoughtful little bastard aren't you. What's all this about?"

Deakin ladled the fried bread onto a plate and sat down opposite Rake. He started to eat.

"I said what's all this about?"

"Just thought you'd appreciate some nourishment; Old Mother Hubbard and all that, just thought, why not? It's in the spirit of the time."

"You lied to me."

Deakin dropped his cutlery onto the plate and sat back.

"Well you did," said Rake nonchalantly. "But then Deakin, you're a compulsive liar, so." Rake continued eating, picking up the crispy bread and sliding an egg on top of it. "Any Daddies?"

"What do you mean lied?"

"You weren't in Tangier for Vogue. They sacked you years ago. So, why were you there, who were you with, were you with Logan Frazer? That sort of thing; Daddies?"

"No, sorry."

Rake cut through the yoke of the egg, it bled beautifully into the bread and he mopped and stabbed, building a kebob of flavour onto the tines, he chewed, nodding appreciatively. Deakin poured whisky and lit a cigarette. Rake let the atmosphere build, he was in no hurry.

Danby had taken H.H. Bender to a lock up in Hither Green and collected a sealed envelope of photographs from the little villain. He'd left him there stranded, shouting the odds because he hadn't picked up any money when he'd been press ganged from the house. Danby continued on to Greenwich, paid off the driver and took a walk along the river to a favourite bench and sat. He took his knife from his coat pocket and released the spring-loaded blade. He sliced through the seal and opened the envelope. He looked at the photographs. He looked over to where the masts of the Cutty Sark stabbed at the lowering grey blue sky, he looked one final time at the images, and then he put them back into the envelope, which he shuffled into his inside pocket. He shook his head to clear it, drew a cigarette from the pack with his teeth and lit it, flicking the spent match out into the mizzle. He thought about Noel Deeming, about their fateful meeting, about their sixteen years of work, the messes he'd sorted and what the future might hold.

## 1944: The Glasshouse, Aldershot

Danby was shuffling along in the lunch line when a couple of bruisers pushed in ahead of the queue. No one said anything, save for some low anonymous grumbles. Danby was irked, but he was in no hurry to eat the slop being served, so he let it go. He'd noticed the new face, a Corporal, busted down to Private apparently, for insubordination or some such, who was up front carrying his tray at his side looking at the unappetizing gruel.

The big lags stepped in front of him, hoisting their trays, lifting their chins about to speak. Without hesitating the new face whacked the lip of his tray upwards under the septum of one of the squaddies and pushed. As the thug went down in a spray of blood and mucus, his oppo put a neck brace on the new lad and heaved him down to the floor. The queue parted immediately, ringing the combatants, shouting and calling out, frenzied, like chimpanzees. Danby pushed his way through the melee and lifting the squaddie's head by his hair he chinned him, but the squaddie carried the lad back with him, forearm still rigid across his windpipe. Danby went in hard this time, breaking the squaddie's nose and forcing him to let go. The new lad was up on his feet, putting the boot in as whistles blew and the crowd dispersed to let the provosts through, truncheons swinging. Danby fought back, the lad alongside him, until they were both brought to their knees as the sticks rained down on their heads, their necks and their shoulders.

When the two men got out of solitary they introduced themselves and the lad invited Danby to look him up, if ever he found himself in Soho or Fitzrovia.

"Anywhere up west son, just mention my name, someone will hook you up, no bother, just ask for Noel Deeming. I'll see you right, I never forget a good turn." And with that he walked away, just a face to nod to in passing, then one day he was gone – back to his regiment and out of Danby's life, or so he thought.

Danby took a long slow stroll up to Westminster Bridge and across it into Soho. By the time he got to the Coach and Horses he was soaked to his marrow. The pub was heaving so he leaned against the bar, making space with his big shoulders and his authority.

"Alright Norman, how's it going?" Danby enquired of the landlord.

"Do I know you?"

"Just being sociable. I'll have a Scotch, straight up, double. John Deakin been about?"

"I told you the other day, I'm not..."

"I know. Scotch, straight up, double."

"I heard you."

Norman Balon poured the drink and walked back along the bar to talk to Jeffrey Bernard. Both men looked toward Danby, Barnard shook his head and looked down at his drink. Danby downed the whisky and banged the glass back on the bar. When Norman looked over, Danby pointed at the glass and indicated for a refill. The landlord walked back, took up the glass and refilled it.

"Don't disrespect the glassware."

"I beg your pardon?" said Danby.

"I said – do not disrespect the glassware."

Danby leaned in towards the landlord, his eyes wide and friendly, a smile spreading across his face.

"Have I upset you?" He raised a hand to quell Norman's response. "No, just hang fire, Norman. Only I seem somehow to have caused some offense. If I have, well I'm sorry, no – I am Norman, I really am. By the way, are you Jewish? I only ask because my guvnor fucking hates Jews. I don't know why, but he does. He's just, what would you call it, antipathetic? He just fucking hates Yids, blind hatred, anyway, unreasonable I call it, naked prejudice, worse than spades he says. His hypothesis is that spades are stupid, but Yids now see, they are devious intelligent inbred heathens, therefore worse than spades, what are just ignorant. Has it's own sort of – what would you call it Norman, logic? Not my businesses of course, but you do look Jewish. The nose, you know, the ears obviously I haven't seen your fucking prick, wouldn't want to would I? Fucking right," he suddenly guffawed. " Why would I?"

Norman was reddening by the second, but unusually he seemed lost for words. The punters either side of Danby were of course shocked, but perhaps, somehow, they were enjoying seeing the infamous "rudest landlord in London", getting some stick. Or maybe, like so many, they were just anti-Semitic, Danby didn't know or care, he was enjoying himself.

"So anyway," he continued. "I'm going to have to go back to him, my guvnor, and tell him that you were very unhelpful, very aloof and very condescending. He will, I'm sure, pop along himself to pay you a little visit. You'll probably recognise him,"

Danby drank off his whisky and thumped the glass down hard on the woodwork. 'His name is Noel Deeming." And with that he turned, signalled an airy "so long", and exited the bar.

Alfie Atkins sat in Deeming's lounge watching television. He felt uncomfortable in the smart blue suit, the shirt with the starched collar and the tie, black knit, like he was at a funeral. He looked at his shoes, Slaney Derby, black – Alfie thought they'd not look out of place affixed to callipers. He looked at his watch, nine twenty, and he'd promised Sophie he'd be round by eight to take her down the Fisherman's for music night. She'd have his bollocks. He heard a noise behind him, sounded like curtains billowing in the breeze, but it was *him* in his silk dressing gown, shuffling along from his bedroom, all tarted up and smelling like an old tom. Alfie stood and smiled.

"Right boss, got to be making a move then."

"Oh really? What, you got somewhere to be, son? Got a date or something? Seeing a polony, that Sadie?"

"Sophie."

"That's right, Sophie. Seeing that Sophie, serious is it? Must be, must be serious if you're rushing off," Deeming looked at the clock. "Mind you, pubs shut soon, you going to stay in with her are you, have a couple of sherbets by the fire, round the old hearth, a cosy evening in, that it?"

"There's a late do up the Fisherman's, bit of a sing song, they got an extension. Said I'd be there, family do like, bit of a tradition, you know, as I missed New Years Eve. I sort of promised."

"Well, after all Alfie, a man's word and all that."

"Right, it's, I just haven't seen her much over Christmas boss, and so I did say."

"No, you shoot off, don't mind me."

"I thought if you don't need me anymore tonight, you know, thought you was getting ready for bed."

"You mean after our late night yesterday? You tired? You look knackered Alfie, you do, and what with the sniffles you shouldn't be out on the town, it's stair rods out there, can't you hear it? We did pull a late one though, didn't we? You put in a good shift last night, boy, I can't deny it."

Alfie hated it when Deeming acknowledged their relationship; it made him feel physically sick, it was almost worse than the actuality of it, the moving of a shadow into the light. The two men stood looking at one another, Deeming fully at ease, Alfie battling to restrain his discomfiture. Deeming cocked his head, smiling. The ticking of the clock seemed to Alfie to be unnaturally loud all of a sudden, he could hear the springs tightening at it approached the chiming of the half hour. He thought about offering to suck Deeming off, but that would likely promote either a session or a beating, or both. The doorbell rang just as the clock started chiming. They continued to look at one another. The clock stopped chiming. A key turned in the lock.

"Just me chief," it was Danby, calling from the hallway. The door closed. Footsteps approached. Danby entered the lounge.

"How we doing then, alright?" Danby walked over to the trolley and fixed himself a drink. "Anyone else, boss?"

"Why not? I'll have a Remy, ta."

"Alfie?" Danby enquired.

"He's off, got a date with a scrubber."

Alfie turned to leave; Deeming sat in one of the big armchairs and took a cigar from the onyx box that rested on an Italianate metal and glass coffee table.

"Leave the keys Alfie, I might be needing the motor," Deeming said.

"I haven't got money for a taxi," Alfie said, somewhat petulantly.

"Get a fucking bus like all the other cunts Alfie, real world, son, real world. Get this Danby, pampered little toe-rag, gets used to driving around at night in the Daimler, gets confused, thinks it's his motor, it's a perk Alfie, comes with conditions."

Danby handed Deeming his Cognac, then he pulled his money clip from his pocket and peeled off two pound notes. He pressed them into Alfie's palm.

"Go on son, it's pissing down get a taxi, have a good night, treat the kid to a Bolognaise or something romantic." He winked and steered Alfie Atkins to the front door, letting him out and taking a deep breath before returning to face Deeming. He sat opposite the man, pulled the envelope from his pocket and dropped it onto the coffee table. Deeming sat forward grunting, picked up the envelope examined it and pushed it into the pocket of his dressing gown.

"It's been opened."

"Has it?"

"I just said."

"I didn't give it any attention, boss. Not my business."

"Didn't you?"

"No, I didn't. Like I say, not my business."

"Well someone opened it. They're stuck together, like they got wet."

"Maybe the Bender's had a group wank, I don't know, I don't give a fuck. You sent me, I went, I got them and I brought them here. Job done."

"What do you mean 'group wank'?"

"A group wank, it was a joke."

"So you did look."

"Boss, I assume they are naughty pictures, I don't know, I assumed they weren't snaps of the Queen Mum at Ascot, I was making a joke."

"I'm not laughing."

"You rarely fucking do, chief."

"You being funny?"

"Clearly not."

"You want to watch that, we might have a falling out you keep sticking your nose in."

"You better be joking."

"Now *you're* not laughing."

Danby put his glass on the coffee table and stood. He looked down at Deeming, holding the man's gaze, holding his nerve, holding everything in.

"Goodnight boss."

"You found Deakin?"

"He's gone underground."

"Better keep looking Danby. I want them negatives, and I want that little twerp where I can have a few words. Did you try David Archer?"

"I'm going home."

"Well nighty night then, son. You toddle off, have a good one, and don't mind me."

Danby turned and walked from the room. Deeming downed his drink and sat back in the chair.

"Don't mind me, none of you, selfish cunts," he said to the world.

## Chapter Five

As dawn broke over the Charing Cross Road the light found Rake sitting on his bed looking over at the sleeping figure of Deakin, who lay snoring on the sofa. The snore had been bothering Rake since he'd awoken in the early hours. It wasn't particularly loud, but it was somehow the worse for that, a popping, puffing sound underpinned by a dreadful wheeze. Now, as the room lifted, Rake could see Deakin's lips blow the breath into the room, accompanied by an occasional chewing motion and a muffled chomping, as if the man was masticating some foul species of offal. Rake sighed and got out of bed. He'd thought about awakening him but, dreadful as the spectacle was, the idea of having to engage with him was too much to bear. The sound of movement disturbed Deakin who turned onto his side, breaking wind as he shifted position. The room was immediately contaminated by a smell so offensive that Rake held his breath and covered his nose and mouth with his hand as he hurried to the hallway, dragging his clothes with him as he headed to the bathroom.

    Rake called Peter Sweet from a phone box and arranged to meet him at the Partisan Coffee House in Carlyle Street at eight thirty. Sweet arrived as Rake was finishing his fry up.

    "Ordered you a breakfast", Rake said.

    "I've eaten guv, sorry."

    "It's good."

    "I couldn't."

Rake shrugged and forked the sausage from Sweet's plate and continued eating.

    "We going to Roy Huff's then, Ladbroke Grove isn't it?" Rake said.

    "Yes, basement flat in Oxford Gardens. He shares, sorry, shared it with Maurice Cohen."

    "Deacon Blood, Deacon Blood, right? The bloke who was supposed to be looking after Huff in Tangier? Tell me about him."

    "Well he's another has been, really. Was in the hit parade a couple of times back in fifty eight, did the U.K. version of "Purple People Eater", but it wasn't big news. Had a hit with "I

Fell For Frankenstein's Bride", that was about it. He moonlights as a bouncer, done a bit of wrestling for Frazer as Deacon Blood, you know, novelty value I suppose."

Rake chewed and nodded, then he forked a rasher of bacon onto his plate and folded it into a slice of bread.

"I'll take it with me," he said as he stood and walked towards the door.

They got to Oxford Gardens at nine thirty five. Number 1A was a garden flat, and having knocked on the door without success they walked round to the French Windows and hammered on the glass. After a few minutes had passed the tatty curtain was pulled back to reveal a behemoth of a man with a gaunt face and a mop of unruly hair, dyed a dingy matt black.

"The fuck you want?" he shouted through the door. Rake pressed his warrant card against the glass. The left door was unlocked and pulled open.

"I said what do you want?"

"Maurice Cohen?"

"And?"

"I'm Detective Chief Inspector Rake, West End Central. This is D.S. Sweet. We're here about Logan Frazer."

"What about him?"

"It's freezing out here Mister Cohen, may we come in?"

"Bit of an early bird aren't you?"

"Justice cannot sleep forever, Mister Cohen."

"Come again?"

"Thomas Jefferson. Anyway, how about we come in out of the cold and have a bit of a chat?" Cohen made a guttural sound, but he stepped back to allow ingress. He loped over to a couch, his head less than two inches from the ceiling. When he sat the couch echoed the mans guttural groan. Rake sat in an armchair while Sweet propped an elbow on the mantelpiece and took out his notebook and pencil.

"As you know, Logan Frazer is dead."

"I fucking hope so, I was at his funeral."

"You may have seen in the papers that he was murdered."

"You what? I haven't seen the papers. What do you mean murdered?"

"He was murdered, then the flat was set ablaze in an attempt to cover up the crime."

"Murdered how?"

"Blunt force trauma – he was hit on the head."

"It came from anger," said Sweet. "His skull was pulped."

"Why's this all coming out now?"

"His body was exhumed, someone in his family wasn't satisfied, apparently," Sweet said. Rake gave a slight shake of his head and Sweet clammed up. They let the silence build.

Cohen poured some brandy into a dirty glass and necked it. His sallow face blanched, then reddened as the alcohol hit his system.

"Who done it?"

"We have no idea at the moment, Mister Cohen. But we are particularly interested in a trip Frazer took to Tangier last November. Something seems to have happened during the holiday, or maybe a number of things, but certainly it seems like an eventful festival, well - you know don't you?"

"You mean Roy?"

"Certainly, Roy and – other things, other people, other shenanigans"

Cohen sat back, holding Rake's eye, waiting, not willing or not able to go further. His almond shaped eyes became hooded, blank, a dead stare – like black stones.

"Shenanigans, is that what it's called?"

"I can see that it's a painful subject," Rake offered.

"You can't see nothing."

"So tell us."

"Tell you what copper, you ask a question and I'll see if I can answer it."

"All right Mister Cohen. Who was staying at the Hotel Continental in November of last year as part of Logan Frazer's cohort?"

"Me, Roy, Charley Goole, Phil Fry and Paddy Gupta."

"Charley Goole, that's Chuck Blizzard, Patrick Gupta is Rocky Saint James, right?" Sweet offered. Cohen nodded.

"Yeah, and Phil is Johnny Rocket."

"How about John Deakin?" Rake asked.

"He was there, not with Frazer as far as I know."

"Was he with anyone?"

"Yeah, some flash ponce, didn't know him, didn't want to, bit of a pillock."

"You mean Larry Parnes?"

"No, I mean he was there old Larry, for the party at Barbara Hutton's palace, but I know that cunt. This was another cunt."

"So you all went to the party?"

"That was the idea, but Roy and the flash Harry and Logan all went off for a puff up on the roof before the shindig."

"A puff?" This was Sweet again.

"Pot, I told Roy not to go, but he was up for it, can't argue with the lad when he's game on. Little bugger, fuck me." Cohen trailed off, a tangible sadness manifesting as his shoulders slumped and his black eyes glassed over like a bird of prey.

"Fuck me," he said again, his words trailing off, yet filling the room.

Rake signalled Sweet to wait, to hold the moment. Silence vacuumed the air from the room. Rake could hear his heart beating. A minute, maybe two ticked by, though it felt like an age.

"Roy got sick, really sick, like – I don't know, I was wondering if it was opium or something. But Logan and the other geezer seemed all right. Anyway. I wanted to hang back, but Logan said me Phil, Charley and Paddy had to go to the do, it was a junket, whatever that is, contracted like. So I put Roy to bed, settled him down, got him to sleep, he seemed fine, you know? He did, sleeping like a baby, put the bin next to his bed like, seemed kosher. So I went. When I come back, early hours - went up to the room, ah fucking hell, fuck me."

"He was dead?" Sweet again, Rake gave him a look.

"Yeah, he was dead. He was dead. He was fucking dead, you cunt, all right?" Again, a protracted silence, but not an absence, a silence full of pain, pain and rage. Eventually Rake leaned forward and spoke, his steady voice filling the room, reverberating and with an edge.

"Let's knuckle down to it Mister Cohen, eh? Whilst you and your pals swanned off to the party, something happened to Roy Huff, your charge, the boy you were supposed to be looking after, right? Something so heinous that he ended up taking his own life. My sense is this, the boy was set up, and he was the other agenda right, am I right? My guess is that he didn't know it, that he was a pawn, but other people did know it, were in the know, right? So my question is, Mister Cohen, were you one of the people in the know? Someone set it up and someone enabled it, what -?"

That was as far as it went, suddenly glass was showering down on Rake and the big man was flying through the space between them, bearing down, his face distorted like a rabid mastiff, teeth bared fingers clutching at air. Rake tried to pull his blackjack from his coat pocket but he was too late, the man covered him like a blanket and they fell together from the chair, rolling onto the floor.

Detective Sergeant Sweet wasn't up to much physically; he wasn't a coward, not exactly. But he was a hesitant man, and he did hesitate rather too long in that instance. This left Rake with very few options, so he took the one that led the shortest route to release. He took hold of Cohen's rather large scrotum and squeezed then twisted, applying pressure through his forearm, his wrist and his fist – and then yanking down hard. The big man's head arched up and back, his eyes reddening and bulging as if to free themselves from their sockets. The veins on his neck stood like ropes against his flushing skin and a strangled yelp escaped his throat like a screaming kettle.

"Cuff him," Rake panted.

Sweet managed to cuff the man's wrists behind him and helped Rake roll him onto his back. Rake stood up and took a walk around the small room, shaking off the trauma. Then he up-righted the chair and sat back down. He lit a cigarette, then, at last, he looked over at Cohen.

"You've got quite a bee in your bonnet, Mister Cohen. Quite a bee."

"I never would have done nothing to hurt that boy."

"I can accept that."

"Am I being nicked?"

"I don't know yet. Shall we see if we can conclude this little interview in a civilised manner?"

Rake signalled to Sweet and together they helped Cohen back onto the couch, though they didn't undo the handcuffs.

"I'm in bloody agony, think you've done me a serious injury."

"Assaulting a police officer is a serious offense, chum. You're a big strapping fellow, you'll survive, I should really pull you in, do it by the book."

"Do what you like, I don't give a toss."

They sat for a while, Cohen holding Rake's eyes, clenching his jaw, his breathing slowly settling.

"Take the cuff's off Sergeant, please," Rake said after a few minutes had passed. Sweet gave a look, hesitated, and then complied. Cohen shook his hands like a minstrel, then rubbed his wrists and relaxed into the couch.

"If you weren't involved, who was?"

"All I know is it wasn't the blokes what went to the do. Can't have been. We went together in a chara, stuck together 'cos we was like fish out of water, like fuckin' freaks at a sideshow, and then we took the chara back to the hotel. When we got there it was all over. Roy, Roy had passed and we was ushered off to be questioned."

"So that leaves who?"

"Roy, Logan and the geezer, poncey bollocks"

"What about Deakin?"

"I can't remember if he was at the party, he wasn't with us. I don't know."

"The post mortem described injuries to Roy Huff consistent with anal penetration, and other injuries sustained, suggesting a sexually motivated, sadistic beating."

"Why are you telling me this? Why are you punishing me? Can't you see? Are you blind?"

"It wasn't reported in detail in the press over here. But it was in some papers on the Continent, in France particularly."

"I don't read the papers here mate, let alone foreign shite," Cohen was getting agitated again.

"I'm not trying to upset you Mister Cohen, I'm just trying to see if Roy's death is possibly linked to Frazer's murder. What do you make of it?"

"I don't know, what am I supposed to know? He got messed up on reefer, had a brainstorm or something. Look, Roy was highly-strung, right; he'd tried it before, cutting hisself I mean, having to have his stomach pumped and that. That's why, that's why I was sharing a room with him, to keep an eye out. That's why Frazer stumped up for this place, for me to watch over the boy. He was the main chance for Frazer, the only one with any real talent. The boy had charisma, and he could sing, and write songs, proper songs I mean, not the garbage they put out, classic ballads and poetry. Here look."

Cohen struggled to his feet and limped over to the sideboard. He came back with a small vellum bound daybook. He sat heavily on the couch and leaned to hand the volume to Rake, as if the book was something rare and of great value. Rake opened the book at a random page and read.

*Well I waited as you willed, waited as the rain fell*
*Waited as it spilled, overflowing from the gutters*
*Rising through the grills, cascading toward the river*
*Carrying me away from you, murmuring – you must forgive her*

Rake closed the book nodding sagely, hiding, he hoped, his critical eye. He handed the book across to Cohen, who collected it and nestled it in his lap. There was something solemn in the air, and Rake found himself suddenly eager to escape the cloying atmosphere. He stood and signalled to Sweet, they headed to the French windows and eased into the garden. Looking back he saw that Cohen was sitting, unmoving, frozen, fondling the book, not registering their departure.

"Any good?" Sweet asked.

"Dreadful juvenilia," Rake led the way along the slippery path. "Was that depressing or am I just depressed? Rhetorical," he said, taking the steps two at a time. When they got to the car Rake turned to face Sweet.

"What was all that about heads getting pulped?"
"What do you mean?"
"I mean what I say."
"I was just trying to open him up, get him going."
"In future, don't – all right?"
"All right, whatever you say, you're the guvnor."
"If his head had been pulped they would not have made the initial mistake at the P.M. – don't assume everybody's stupid, they're not."
"Cohen is."
"Is he? Get in, I'm cold."

Sweet opened the door and climbed in, and then he reached across to open the passenger door. Get in then if you're cold, you lanky string of piss, he thought to himself. "I'll keep my mouth shut in future and just take notes and type reports and drive the fucking car, sir – okay?" is what he actually said.

"Don't pout, it's unseemly."

Sweet turned the engine over and drove in silence to Savile Row, to type up the report.

Danby climbed the steps of Piccadilly Tube as the milky sun began to dip. He walked along Shaftsbury Avenue, turned left up Dean Street and then right onto Old Compton Street. He stopped off at Wheeler's and ate a meal of Dover Sole and French fries accompanied by a glass of Champagne, waiting for a time when he thought the shop would be shut. Satisfied he walked into the inky dark of that glacial evening, turned right onto Greek Street and stood watching David Archer shut up his bookshop. When Archer moved into the back room, Danby walked across the street and tapped on the glass. David Archer ambled to the door smiling. He shrugged apologetically and pointed to his watch, offering a sorrowful lifting of his eyebrows followed by a sad shake of his head. Danby mumbled a few words. Archer put his hand behind his ear, mouthing "Sorry?" Danby mimed something that spoke of urgency, keeping the deceptively open not to say

56

chummy expression that he had rehearsed so often in his mirror. David Archer unbolted the door and opened it wide.

"I'm so sorry," he said. "I've cashed up. Can I help you?"

"Hello David," Danby said. "John asked me to pop round."

"John?"

"Let's step inside, shall we?"

Danby lightly pushed past Archer and walked toward the back room. David Archer closed the door, but this time he didn't bolt it, he was shaking his head, he looked prissy to Danby. Danby never had liked prissy men.

Danby had a great many aversions and didn't take to David Archer: the mimsy mouth, the tight wavy hair, the tortoiseshell glasses, and the shabby primness of his suit. Seedy pouf, he thought to himself. It made it easier, it always made it easier. Archer turned to follow Danby, his body language demonstrating the intention to take back some kind of personal agency in his shop. *His* shop. His space. His living. His life.

"About John?" he said, his plummy tone projecting a born authority.

"He asked me to collect a few of his belongings. I've to drop them round to wherever he's staying, though, to be honest David, he forgot to tell me the exact address, said you'd be able to give me directions."

"So he has actually moved out then?"

"Oh no, no, he's not moved out. It's temporary, as I understand it. From what John said, he said – he implied a temporary estrangement, more of a sabbatical, just needs to sort his bonce out. You know John, well, of course you do. Nice shop."

"Thank you."

"What sort of shop would you call it?"

"Pardon?"

"I said, what sort of shop would you call it?"

"Why, it's a book shop, and a press."

"What do you mean, a press?"

"We publish."

"What, dirty books?"

"By no means. Look, who are you? If John want's his belongings he can damn well come himself. Not that he has much

57

in the way of belongings. I do have some of his photography, stuffed in boxes under the bed, and possibly some clothes, not much. He hasn't much, has he? Are you a friend, he's never spoken of you?"

" Oh, I'm his friend, bosom buddies, old pals. Let's go and get the photo's."

"Look, I just told you, if John wants anything he's most welcome to come and pick them up. Now then, I need to lock up the shop. Is there anything else I can do for you?"

"Yes cunty," said Danby, before he jabbed David Archer in the stomach, just above the bottom button of his waistcoat.

# Chapter Six

Rake was tired, tired to his bones, to his marrow. Work had never seemed peripheral to life, but now there was no life, no wife, no hope, and no joy – just work, all encompassing. He felt as if he'd drawn his fist down into his bowels and pulled himself inside out. He just wanted to get back to his room, yet he hated that room, and now Deakin was there, stinking it up, fouling it up. He needed a holiday, or maybe just a weekend – somewhere, some other place, a world away from the Charing Cross Road.

He shuffled up the stairs, fishing for his key. But the door was ajar, the woodwork splintered at the jamb by the mortice. Gingerly he pushed the door. It creaked open – he'd not noticed the creak before, it seemed unnaturally loud. He stepped inside, holding the key between his index and second finger like a spike. The room was dissembled, upended, overturned. He called out for Deakin, nothing. He stepped into the kitchenette, more chaos. He walked back onto the landing, calling once more for Deakin. He looked at his watch; it was nearing ten past ten. He shouldn't have stopped off at Muriel's; he shouldn't have drunk so much, he shouldn't have moved on to the French. Rake shook his head to clear it. It didn't work. He walked back to his room and pushed the door shut, but it slowly opened again, ushering ghosts. He summoned methodology and shaking off his coat he began a search of the room. Noting cigarette butts on the floor he wrapped his handkerchief around his fingers and lifted the heavy cut glass ashtray. There was blood. Muttering a curse Rake continued the search. Finally he sat on the edge of the bed.

He was caught in a subterfuge. If he rang it in he'd have to explain why a notorious homosexual reprobate was hiding out in his flat. He'd be for it, again. His own past held for examination, the rumours underpinned by the very fact of the association. Yet he knew Deakin was almost certainly dead or being held somewhere out of reach. The blood drained from his head and he fell backwards onto the bed, trying to steady his breathing. The room spun and he gripped the mattress for dear life.

"It's just the drink," he blurted. Then the doorbell rang.

Danby held his head under the tap and watched the water run red. Straightening, he pressed the flannel against the wound on the back of his scalp and walked to his bedroom and sat on the Lloyd Loom chair that abutted his bed. The bastard wouldn't stop bleeding. His shirt was a Rorschach test, red upon white, he stripped it off, his vest was stained, so he pulled it over his head, picked up his tumbler and drank off the Scotch, letting the warm blood turn cold on his clavicle where it puddled.

"Little rat," he said. Then the doorbell rang.

Rake shot up, swayed, and then pulled the rattling sash up, calling out for Deakin, but he remembered then that the little man had a key. He heard the hollow click clacking of heels in the alleyway, then a woman stood in the lamplight looking up at him as fat globules of rain fell on her face and into her eyes.

"Wait, wait there a minute." He went to his coat and fished out his key, then he went back to the window, half expecting her to be gone, or maybe to have been a phantom. But there she stood, waiting. He dropped the key out into the rain. She caught it expertly and he walked back into the debris of his room. He looked about him, but there was too much disorder to clear away so he went to the little mirror in the kitchenette and tidied his hair as her footsteps ascended the stairway.

Danby pulled on his jacket over his naked torso and opened the door. He knew who it would be; no one else knew where he lived. Deeming stood there with Alfie Atkins. Deeming nodded and walked past Danby into the cramped living room.

"You coming in?" Danby said to Alfie.

"He can wait in the motor," Deeming said over his shoulder.

Danby shut the door and followed Deeming into the room. Deeming took off his overcoat and handed it to Danby.

"Put it on a hanger, it's wet."

Danby went into the bedroom with the coat, put it on a hanger and hung it on the bedroom door. Shrugging off his jacket he pulled open a drawer and took out a sweater, pulling it over his head and reopening the wound. Back in the living room he poured two whiskies and handed one to Deeming. They sat opposite one another, both men took a sip then Deeming lifted his chin questioningly.

"Yes?" Danby asked, though it was of course obvious.

"Been in the wars?"

Danby nodded. He sipped - Deeming mirrored him. His dead black eyes were rimmed in red and a vein pulsed in his temple. He rested his tumbler on the arm of the chair.

"Am I goin' to have to drag it out of you? I've been waiting for a phone call."

"I was busy, you can see."

"So?"

"I haven't got the negatives, not yet."

Deeming kept on looking, the vein kept on pulsing, Danby wasn't going to allow the conversation to turn into an interrogation; he didn't see this as part of his job, not really. Yet he had to admit, he had been made to look foolish, so he shrugged and leaned back in his chair.

"I found Deakin. I went to his boyfriend's shop, pulled a couple of strokes, had to get a bit heavy actually. Anyway, he had some photos and negatives, but all old stuff, fashion plates, some stuff in Italy or whatever, nothing of interest to you. But I got an address on the Charing Cross Road where he's been staying."

"Whose gaff?"

"I don't know, just a couple of rooms above a book shop. So I went, waited until some old geezer came out, nipped in, boshed my way into the flat, and - "

"And?"

"There was Deakin."

She walked into the room. Rake didn't quite know what to do with himself, with his body, what shape to make. He sat down on the bed, then sprung up and offered Ruth a seat at the table. She stood looking about her. Then she looked straight into his eyes and smiled, the smile turning downward almost immediately as the tears and the sobs burst through.

"Sorry, sorry," she heaved. "Don't be nice to me, please."

Rake guided his wife into a seat and looked about for the remnants of a drink. He couldn't even see the empties. He went to the sink and poured water into a mug. He handed it to her and sat, resting his hand lightly on hers. She drew her hand away as if she'd been scalded.

"I said don't be nice to me!"

Deeming waved his tumbler and Danby refilled it and sat back in his armchair.

"Continue, why don't you?" Deeming said.

"He said that the negatives weren't in the place, so I looked, took a good look about. Didn't find anything."

"So?"

"So, while I was looking little cunt came up behind me and crowned me."

"Resourceful."

"You could say that."

"What would you call it?"

Danby nodded. The blood was trickling uncomfortably down his neck. He wanted to get a handkerchief, but he could wait. He'd better wait. This wasn't over. Not by a long chalk.

She sat there at the mean little table in the tatty room until her tears dried on her cheeks and the mucus began to crust about her nostrils.

"I must look a mess," she laughed and gulped and shivered all at once.

"What happened?"

"He said I'd driven him mad, that I've driven all my," she trailed off, "you know. I just think he got bored, if I'm honest."

"You've always been honest, Ruth. To a fault."

She laughed again and looked at him through her thick wet eyelashes.

"We were having supper at Toscana, he left me there, so I came here, I haven't any money Cyril, I'm so sorry. I didn't know what else to do."

"It's not a problem. I have money, I'll get you home, don't worry about it."

There was a prolonged and rather awkward silence. Rake found that he couldn't quite catch his breath. He was aware of a building flatulence and was worried lest it managed a noisome escape. He shifted in his seat and let go of a silent fart. He waited to see if it was rank, but felt he'd got away with it.

"I'd rather stay, Cyril. I don't expect anything, just a cuddle. Just a cuddle."

He reddened, he knew that he should not capitulate, that the massive dune that he had climbed since leaving her, would turn to quicksand in a moment.

"No love, no, I'm sorry. I'll just nip to the lavatory and then I'll get you a taxi."

"Cyril," she whispered.

He stood and walked swiftly to the door and out to the landing, letting off tiny squeaks with each step. He sat on the lavatory and fully evacuated in one thrusting explosion of relief.

"Rake, Rake come on," he muttered. "Big boy, big bad boy, fuck it, don't fucking need it. Don't need it, didn't ask for it, don't want it. No, no, absolutely no." He wiped himself and flushed the toilet. He washed his hands and wiped them on his trousers. When he entered the room again, she was standing in the centre by the foot of the bed.

"I know what you need, Cyril. I know what you've missed," she said.

Then she turned and lifted her skirt. She had no panties on. Her bottom was fully exposed to him. Rake let out a low throaty moan and fell immediately to his knees. He poked his tongue high into her anus, and then he bit her buttock, his hands scrambling to undo his fly buttons. His penis was immediately engorged with blood and he began to pull on it like a monkey, all the while guttural sounds escaped him as the fierce pumping escalated. She leaned forward onto the bed, holding herself up with one arm, using her left hand to spread her buttock cheek, pushing into his face.

"Can you smell me?"

He grunted in assent. He licked and lapped at her, then pulled back; spread her buttocks wide, eyeing her anus, watching it dilate. Then he pushed her down on the mattress so that she was on all fours. He slapped her buttocks hard. Then he pushed his cock into her arse and watched as it slid out, almost to the tip, then he thrust deeply into her. He lay on top of her as they fucked; she was like a bridge, strong and hard. He reached around her, pulling her breasts from her dress, ripping the bra down so that he could grasp and knead her. He came suddenly, arching up and back, pushing her head into the blanket. His penis softened immediately and slid from her anus. She farted loudly and semen spat from the orifice and settled on the back of her thigh.

"You remember how we met?" Noel Deeming took a long pull on his cigar, his eyes had not left Danby's, not for a second. "Back then, back there in Aldershot, remember? I thought you were the dog's bollocks. Fuck me, those two big chaps in the lunch queue, pushing in, fronting me up like I was a cunt. I was getting a right seeing to, then ta da – there you was, steaming in, fucking hell," he shook his head, coughing out a laugh.

"I remember," Danby said.

"You were magnificent, honest, straight up, diamond. Then, where was it?"

"Dog and Duck."

"Dog and Duck, Frith Street, yeah, what fifty one?"

"'bout then."

"Must have been, nineteen fifty, fifty one. I was having bother with the Maltese firm, right? Still don't know the details, but well – what can I say?"

Danby got up, took Deeming's glass, refilled it and topped up his own, and then he sat back down and crossed his legs, waiting. Deeming nodded a "cheers" and sipped his drink, savouring the liquor expansively.

"What's this, Irish?"

"Jameson."

"I'm more of a Scotch single malt man, but you know that - for next time. Anyway, so the Maltese, you cleared them out, what – single-handed? Yeah, single handed, like I say don't know the details, don't need to I'm what they call a delegator, I'm not middle management, I delegate. Job well done, no – definitely, job well done. Then, let me think, the kike twins, the Yids. Helped me reach an accommodation, smoothed things over," he shook his head as if conjuring a fond reminiscence, then he dropped his cigar into his drink, it fizzled. "Don't like Irish, for future reference. Then it was them brothers, Charlie and thingy, you know, the scrap metal merchants south of the river, pikey cunts, can't remember – oh, the Richardson's, them. You blew them up, I don't remember, anyway, what's my point?"

"I don't know, what is your point?"

"Help me out, son. I'm not being rhetorical."

"I did good work," Danby deadpanned.

"That's it, *did*. Who said – you're only as good as your last whatsit?"

"You did."

"Did I, me? Did I? That'd be right, eh?"

"I'm tired, boss, I want to get to bed."

"Tired? Are you? Probably got a concussion, you're looking wan, is that a word? It is yeah - wan. You look pasty, that's a lovely word, like pastry, Mister Pastry, you look Pastry, you look like Mister Pastry. What's his name?"

"Richard Hearne."

"You know a lot."

There was a tension now, like catgut being stretched and twanging, reverberating in Danby's head over and over, making him feel nauseous, he lit another cigarette. It didn't help.

"Get to the fucking point, I'm going to my bed," the twang turned to tinnitus which morphed into a thumping in his temples, a harbinger of restless anger which had to be avoided, lest it explode. Deeming tilted his head, still holding eye contact. His mouth turned down sourly.

"You need to watch that, indeed you do, son. All right, let us get down to the nub. You was all that, but I'm starting to wonder. You let some little pouf get the better of you tonight. I'm getting the feeling you're not putting your back into it. You're not using elbow grease, as my old mum used to say, silly old cunt that she was. Fucking whore. You're being slipshod, she said that too, cunt. You know that Mister Pastry was Richard whatsit, but you can't be bothered to sort out my rather urgent predicament.

If you don't want the job, well fair do's, but you're taking my money aren't you, right? I'm fucking paying you for services fucking rendered aren't I? But you're not fucking rendering them, right, are you? You are my employee, I am your employer, and I have actually in actual fact delegated to you a simple bit of business. Now, and this is very difficult for me, but I feel in all conscience that it has to be said, if you want your employment terminated by all means, no hard feelings blah blah, I'll take the keys to this lovely apartment, have the keys to the nice motor and you can fuck off tonight. Simple."

"If I go, boss, it'll be on my terms," Danby said evenly. He stood and looked down at Deeming. "I underestimated Deakin, I did. So now it's personal. I'll get your pictures and I'll sort him out. Or you can delegate it to some other cunt. Up to you."

"That's more like it, fire in the belly. Good boy, just make it soon, alright?"

Danby nodded and walked towards his bedroom, the tension slowly settling in his head, like a receding train in a tunnel. He returned with the overcoat and draped it over the arm of the chair.

"Goodnight," he said. He went back into the bedroom.

"I'll see myself out," Deeming called. He looked back as the bedroom door closed. Then he tipped the drink from the arm of the chair, watching as the stain and ash spread on the carpet. He nodded with satisfaction. Alfie Atkins was going to get a proper work out tonight.

Rake went into the kitchenette and took a tea towel from the hook by the sink. He walked back to the bedroom and wiped semen from Ruth's thigh. He dropped the cloth onto the floor and adjusted his fly buttons, and then he sat at the table and lit a cigarette.

"Got one for me?" Ruth said, stretching, turning, and shuffling her bottom to the edge of the mattress. She kicked off her shoes, not a good sign, he thought. Nevertheless, he took a cigarette from the pack, went to her and lit it. She nodded and inhaled deeply. She patted the mattress.

"Come, sit here beside me. I could do with one of your lovely cuddles. How about you get comfy and I'll give you a nice massage, you look so tense, didn't that help?" She lay back down, resting her head on her hand, looking up at him.

"Sweetheart, I'm going to get you a taxi, you're going home."

"It's so late and I'm really sleepy. I could sleep for a week, honestly, just to feel your arms around me, you used to say that waking up with me was like Christmas every day."

"That was a long time ago Ruth, a lifetime ago. Finish the cigarette, I'll nip out and get you a taxi, it's best."

"Best for you, not for me."

"I know what will happen. We'll fight, you'll start and we'll fight."

"Not tonight, I'm so tired I could sleep standing up."

"But you won't, Ruth. It'll get to the early hours and then it'll just start up again and honestly, love, I can't face it. I'm not good, in myself I mean, I'm up to my chin in it and I need to be on my own tonight."

"Oh, so you just needed a fuck, is that it? Better than a wank, was I?"

"Don't talk like that, it isn't like that. I just, I really need to get to bed and be ready for the morning."

"You need, you need, what about what I need? You expect me to sit in a taxi all the way to Putney, smelling like this, like a dirty tom? I've been through hell tonight, I'm vulnerable, I'm in a very vulnerable state Cyril. I'm upset; I came to you for comfort. You hate me, I can see it in your eyes, you despise me, don't you?"

"Ruth, of course I don't, but we're separated."

"No, no – you left me, you walked out and left me."

"I was frightened, love. I was frightened," God he sounded tired, and like he was wheedling, horrible.

"Frightened of what, darling?"

"Frightened I was going to kill you! You never stop; you never stop – even to draw breath. I ended up having to talk so loudly that even I couldn't make out what I was trying to say. I was going mad, literally."

"But I forgave you, Cyril – for all the shouting, and for when you hurt me."

"I didn't hurt you, I didn't – what do you mean, hurt you?"

"I always said, you don't know your own strength, I know you didn't mean to, but you hurt me."

"I retrained you, I restrained you – to stop you running off into the night. Oh love, look – it's happening - it's happening already, Christ almighty!"

"Then let's just snuggle up in bed and go to sleep, please. Just a lovely snuggle, like we used to. I'll give you a massage and you can fall asleep. Shall we try?"

"No – absolutely not. I'm going to go and get you a taxi and you'll go home. I'll wait up and just please telephone me to let you know you're home safe."

Ruth swung herself from the bed; she swayed slightly, gathered herself and slipped into her shoes. She was blind with fury and frustration. He moved to help her, but she flung her palms toward him, pushing at the fetid air, fending him off. She searched for her coat, found it on the floor by the table and slung it over her shoulder.

"I'll go and get the taxi," he was pleading now, he could hear it in his own voice and it made him sick.

"Oh bugger off, just – you," she shuddered and headed to the broken door. She yanked it fully open and slammed it violently shut. It swung back on its hinges. He followed her onto the landing and watched as she stumbled down the stairway, slapping her hand on the wall with each faltering step.

"At least take some money, please Ruth."

"Fuck your money," she shouted, her words echoing up to him. Someone shouted from behind a closed door for them to shut up. He heard the front door open. It didn't close – he ran down the stairs after his wife, following her into the night, abandoning himself to the quicksand of their broken marriage.

# Chapter Seven

Rake stood at the window, a cup of coffee going cold in his hand. She was sound asleep; lying spread-eagled in the bed, snoring fitfully. He'd managed to cajole her back to the flat after the familiar pantomime: the screaming, the shouting, the stamping, the crying – and him, acting like a damn priest, firm but gentle, like a bhikkhu. It was like a sodden blanket being laid on a fire. The louder she became the quieter was his response, though of course, he felt like murdering her. Once she had fallen asleep he had tidied the flat, washed and dressed in clean clothes and looked for clues. There were none. He watched as the Wolsey pulled up to the kerb. The horn sounded in two short bips, and so he turned, put the cup on the table, walked through the hanging door and descended the stairs.

    Sweet pulled away as soon as Rake had settled in his seat. They drove past Regents Park heading toward Camden Town. Neither man had spoken after a curt hello, which suited Rake. He burped coffee into his mouth and swallowed it down. He felt as though he was falling apart. Deakin and then Ruth, he hadn't slept for days. His pulse hadn't dropped below one twenty he was sure, he could feel it, like a klaxon racing through his temples, bursting in his chest. He worked to control his breathing. He had barbiturates back at the flat, he'd get rid of her tonight, somehow – and it was his day off tomorrow.
    "Which one is this?" he asked.
    "The Paki."
    "Patrick Gupta?"
Sweet nodded and turned the car right onto Fitzroy Road. Sweet slowed, looking at numbers, then he pulled up and switched off the engine.
    "Rocky Saint James, twenty two, in the charts at the moment – so is doing better than that bastard Tweak."
    "Maybe he's got some talent, " Rake proffered.
    "Flash in the pan."

They climbed out of the car and went to the front door. Neither man had commented on the Standard Vanguard that had followed them at a distance from the Charing Cross Road.

Danby watched the two men enter the building then he flicked his cigarette out of the window of the Vanguard and sat for a couple of moments, thinking. He checked his watch: nine thirty. The sky was clearing; it was going to be a fine, crisp winters day. A welcome change after all the rain. He got out and trotted through traffic to the telephone box on the corner of Chalcot Road. He dialled, keeping the house in view. The ringing stopped and he heard Deeming's gruff, phlegmy baritone over the wires, he pressed the button and the coins clattered to the floor of the box.

"It's me. Look I've got to be quick; I waited outside the gaff that Deakin was holed up in. There was a bloke standing up at the window of the room, been there a long time, so anyway, I've followed him up to Camden, yes definitely him. What? Right, listen, unmistakable, no – no, I don't know him. Listen, thing is, he's a cozzer." There was a long silence. Danby pushed a couple of coins into the box. Then Deeming was back on the line. Danby shifted his position, rifling through his pockets for cigarettes, but he'd left his lighter in the Vanguard.

"What do you want - ? Yes, all right, I'll follow them back - yes there are two of them, I'll follow them back to find out if they go to a station, right? Then you can perhaps use your contacts to - Well if you know which station he's at. No boss, I looked, of course, no name on the bell at the flat, I - " The line went dead. The pips hadn't sounded, so obviously Deeming had hung up.

"Cunt!" Danby said aloud as he placed the receiver back in its cradle and pushed the heavy door open.

"Who's a cunt Mister Danby? " said the tall, gaunt man who stood waiting outside the telephone box. It was the man at the window above the bookshop on the Charing Cross Road. Danby was immediately his cool, calm and collected self. He mumbled an apology, keeping his head low and stepping aside to pass the policeman. But the copper mirrored his movement, blocking him. Danby looked at him now, taking him fully into his memory for future reference. He smiled, open and engaging, another face he'd rehearsed in his mirror.

"Want to dance, sweetheart?"

"The name's Rake, ducks, Detective Chief Inspector Rake."

"In a hurry," Danby said, turning to walk away, heading north towards Primrose Hill. Rake skipped a couple of steps and grabbed Danby by his coat, swinging him round and pushing him back against some railings. Danby tensed and resisted. Rake cuffed the man's hat from his head and slapped him backhanded across his face.

"You want to watch that," Danby said, his jaw clenched.

"You'll stand for it," said Rake.

Patrick Gupta had welcomed the policemen into his flat, offering tea. Rake asked if he could use the telephone. He rang through to the station, gave the phone number and requested a trace on a Standard Vanguard BRA 36. They rang back with details within five minutes, Sweet looking confused throughout. Rake asked Gupta if there was a back door, slipped out and was waiting at the telephone box when the expletive was delivered along with the big wedge of the man who had uttered it.

"You'll stand for it," said Rake as he patted Danby down. He hesitated at a pocket, reached in and pulled out a nice set of custom made brass knuckles.

"You the lad that wrecked my flat? Seen a wee scrotum that was idling there? Well? Who are you working for? Come on son, might as well." They heard a door slam and Danby's eyes flicked along to Gupta's building. Rake turned and saw Sweet heading along the pavement towards them. Rake gritted his teeth and slipped the knucks into his pocket.

"Righto, you can cut," he said, smoothing Danby's coat. Danby raised his eyebrows momentarily, and then he turned smartly and walked swiftly away. Sweet met Rake as he walked slowly back toward Gupta's home.

"What's that about?" Sweet said, watching as Danby disappeared around the corner.

"Nothing."

"Didn't look like nothing."

"I thought he was following us, turns out he wasn't. Just a salesman or something, forget it, how are you getting on with Rocky?"

"Just another poncey twerp, makes a proper cup of tea though, must be said."

Rake nodded and they walked together into the flat, Rake cursing the day he'd allowed John Deakin into his life, Sweet beginning to think he was attached to a very strange DCI, and preparing to disassociate himself from the partnership with alacrity. He was building a case for a swift divorce, and he knew exactly who to take it to.

Patrick Gupta made a fresh cup of tea for Rake and offered a tin of Playbox biscuits to the detectives.

"I got them for Christmas from a fan, I don't eat sweet things," he said in a cultured, over enunciated tone that irritated Sweet unreasonably.

"More of a curry man, eh?" Sweet said.

"I have to watch my figure," replied Gupta, without obvious offense. "I have a tendency to run to fat."

"That wouldn't do, would it?" Sweet said.

"So you were saying," this was Rake. "About Tangier?"

"It was a funny situation, as I described to your colleague. It felt a bit, I don't know quite how to describe it really."

"Try," said Rake.

"It felt staged. As though, as though everyone was playing a part. Everyone except poor Roy, that is. Before the party, in the bar after supper, there was Roy, John Deakin, Logan, Larry Parnes and us."

"Which us?"

"Phillip, Charlie, Morrie Cohen and me."

"What about Elmo Tweak?"

"Oh no, no – Kenny wasn't there. He's on the out, no not poor old Kenny."

"Anyone else?"

"Yes, later on, after we'd eaten. This other chap turned up."

"Who invited him?"

"I honestly have no idea. He seemed to know Larry and Logan, oh – and he knew Deakin, I think. They acted as if they were strangers, very odd."

"But they weren't?"

"No, they knew each other, it was quite obvious."

"Obvious?"

"Deakin kept giving him looks, you know, seeking approval. I'm not sure if anyone else noticed, except Morrie of course, very protective of Roy, that one. Anyway, when Morrie went to powder his nose this chap and Logan disappeared with Roy. When Morrie came back he went ballistic, had a dreadful tantrum. And when Roy returned he was obviously the worse for wear, so he went off to bed and we all departed for the delights of Mother Hutton's night of magic at the Palace, dreadful party, nasty people. It was horrible, desperate. Jaded and faded as they say."

"Who says?" Sweet inquired.

"Them!" Gupta replied, giving Sweet a surprisingly firm look. "So anyway, that's about it." Sweet looked over to Rake, shut his notebook and dropped it into his pocket.

"We haven't finished," Rake said pointedly and Sweet took out the notebook, sighing rather impatiently. "Have you any thoughts as to why Huff killed himself?"

"Oh, I don't know, no. I mean, he'd tried it before, he was quite histrionic, which went over well on stage – the whole Johnny Ray thing in performance, but he really was like that, untamed you might say. The only difference between Roy and Little Mickey was that Little Mickey Magnet could command a stage, but Roy wasn't in command of even himself. I mean, when Phil takes off the Johnny Rocket leathers he could be a librarian, but Roy really was crazy, chaotic. He was Little Mickey, in and out of the spotlight."

"Did he have a girlfriend?" Rake asked.

"He wasn't allowed to have a girl, the fans would have gone potty. No, none of us have girlfriends, not officially anyway."

"What about his relationship with Maurice Cohen?"

"What about it?"

"Were they intimate?"

"Morrie loved Roy like a son, but Roy found it stifling, Morrie clucking around him like a mother hen, it was ridiculous, laughable, but there you go, Logan insisted – Roy was only fifteen when Logan took him on, he needed looking after."

"I bet," said Sweet.

"Pardon?"

"The kid was raped, the night he died," said Sweet. "Any thoughts about who might have fancied having a pop? The boy was drugged, pissed up – not what I call being looked after, more like stitched up, more like sacrificed!"

"I can't comment on that."

"Why not?" Sweet asked.

"I was at the party, it was all over when we got back to the Continental, all over in that Roy was dead.'"

"Convenient," Sweet suggested.

"No, not convenient, just factual."

"This other chap, the one who just turned up, were you introduced?" Rake interjected.

"No, he just – he was just there, as though it was a coincidence, I didn't take much notice of him if I'm honest. He just sat there, sweating in his suit. He seemed, I don't know, sort of alien, out of place, not sociable."

"So you didn't catch a name?"

"No, sorry – I didn't."

"Can you describe him?"

"Big, big physically and sort of – well powerful I suppose, he had a dark aura, gave me the willies."

"Gave you the willies?" Sweet said. "What's an aura, like a smell?"

"Everyone has an aura, Sergeant, yours is black, and his was brown."

"What does brown signify?" Rake asked.

"Greed, self love – not particularly attractive."

"What about black?" This was Sweet.

"Anger, ill health perhaps, unresolved trauma certainly."

"Anything else, about the man?" Rake said.

"He had combed his hair to cover a bald patch, and it was dyed, dyed black."

When Danby walked into Muriel's it was already lively, despite the hour. Alfie Atkins was getting a great deal of unwanted attention from a tall horse faced man who Danby didn't recognise, and Deeming was looking vexed, so Danby put his arm around Alfie's shoulder and guided him to where the big man was propped.

"Go and wait in the car," Deeming said to Alfie Atkins. "Go on, fucking disgrace."

Alfie nodded and wended his way through the throng; horse face shrieking in disappointment. He glowered at Deeming then focused his attention back to the two sailors that were hanging off him. Danby ordered a Scotch and water and leaned in to speak.

"Anything?"

Deeming shook his head, Deakin was gone; he could feel it. Danby had blown the chance, letting himself get suckered by that little rat. You couldn't trust anyone nowadays, not to get a job done properly. If you want a job done properly, boy – do it yourself. The words trilled in his brain, nagging and triumphant, the old bitch, always getting the final say, belittling him, scolding him, fingering grease from the stove and sticking it in his face – *I told you to clean the kitchen, you useless little gobshite.*

"Let's get out of this karzy," he said.

As they brushed past horse face Deeming reared at him and the man fell back in shock. One of they sailor boys squared up to Deeming. Danby tweaked the lad's upper lip and pulled him double as Deeming lit out through the door and down the narrow stairway. Danby let go of the boy's lip and wiped his hand down the lad's pea coat.

"You're barred, the pair of you," Muriel shot at Danby. He tapped his brim in a salute and went down the stairs and onto Dean Street. He let Deeming march on ahead. He'd decided not to mention the cozzer fronting him up, he thought: why add insult to injury? It was dark now, and cold after the cloudless day, sharp and inky black with the scent of ozone under the billowing clouds of exhaust. They turned onto Bateman Street and saw Alfie sitting in the motor. Deeming signalled and turned into the Dog and Duck. Alfie cut the engine and climbed out of the Daimler. Danby pulled out a pack of Pall Mall and offered one to Alfie, who nodded and they shared Danby's lighter, blowing vapour into the night air.

"He's copped a right strop," Alfie said, his teeth chattering slightly.

"Well, he's worried."

"What about?"

"You'd better ask him."

"Yeah right," Alfie chuckled.

"Not your place?"

"What do you think?"

"You should turn it in, son – move on."

"And do what? Be a fucking clerk, work in a shop? All I can do is drive."

"So, be a driver."

"What about you mate? Why do you put up with him?" Danby thought about this. He wasn't sure what an exit policy would look like. Terminating his contract might be too literal, it would probably be too literal for Alfie, yes definitely, a sight too literal for Alfie Atkins. He flicked his cigarette into the street and walked into the bar followed by Alfie. They found Deeming in the corner, sitting at a table by the fire. Danby brought a round of drinks and they all sat in silence for a few minutes smoking. When Deeming spoke he spoke quietly, his tone even and admonitory.

"What do you call that then?"

Neither Alfie nor Danby were sure to whom the question was directed, so they snatched a glance at one another and waited. Deeming continued:

"That in there, in the Colony? What was I supposed to think? You Alfie, flirting with that John Minton, lanky string of piss, showing me up, making a show of yourself with that fairy, I was humiliated, I felt – well, it was a fucking slap in the face."

"You've got the wrong end of the stick, boss," Danby said. "The geezer was showing out, Alfie was just being polite."

"Fucking polite you cunt! Is that what you calls it? Fucking polite, fuck me, he was all but showing his arse to the cunt, you berk. What, you two been working on this out in the street? Conspiracy is it? Leave me sitting here drinkless while you two come up with that – oh, you've got the shitty end of the fucking stick, he was just being friendly – he's becoming a bleeding rent boy, looking for new openings, he's forgotten who butters his bread, this one, this – this *ingrate*. No, no – not happening, take me for a mutt, what? Give me the keys; come on, " Deeming slapped his palm on the table then held it out, beckoning. "Come on, you little slag, you can fucking walk back to Ilford, fucking tart."

Alfie dropped the keys into Deeming's hand and the man stood looking down at Danby. Then he tossed the keys to him.

"You drive, think I'm leaving you here with him? I should coco."

Danby took the wheel heading down towards Shaftsbury Avenue. Deeming was pouting, looking out of the passenger window. The atmosphere was intensified in the small space, so Danby cracked his window.

"Want me to freeze?"
Danby wound the window closed. They approached Piccadilly Circus, neon advertisements lit the sky: Cinzano, Smoke Players, CocaCola, Max Factor and Gordon's Gin, illuminating people buses and taxi's in an unworldly silken glow.

"Where?" Danby inquired.
"Home."
Danby turned up Regent Street. He thought he'd better offer something up, if not quite the whole truth, at least a morsel.

"I found out about that copper, the one in the flat."
Deeming didn't respond, not giving an inch, not rewarding the begging dog. "I collared his neighbour. He's a Chief Inspector, name of Rake." Danby stole a sidelong glance as he turned onto Maddox Street. "I didn't get why he'd be shielding Deakin, the neighbour didn't know Deakin. He and Rake don't see much of one another." He drove through to the car park and turned the engine off.

"Want me to come in?"
Deeming shifted round to look at him. He opened his door, the courtesy light made him look orange, sickly, his eyes as black as jet.

"Go and find Alfie, bring him back."
"Did you hear what I said?"
"Did you hear what *I* fucking said?"
"He'll be heading home, or to his bird, could be anywhere."

"Bring him back," Deeming said. He got out, slammed the door and disappeared into the building. Danby executed a three-point turn and nosed the motor south eastwards, down past Berkley Square towards the river. Might as well take the scenic route, he thought, I've got time.

Rake filled in his report and went straight from the station to his flat. The lights and the electric fire were on full blast, but Ruth had gone. He looked around for a note; there wasn't one, so he rang the house, no answer. He sat and smoked a cigarette then rang again; still no answer. He opened the bottle of whisky he'd brought and looked for his phenobarbital - but he couldn't find them, so he started tidying his flat, taking slugs of alcohol at regular intervals. At ten fifteen he started feeling tired, he tried ringing Ruth again – still getting no response, and so he undressed and climbed gratefully into bed. Sleep came immediately, like a welcome guest at a dreary party.

Danby parked outside The Fisherman's Arms on Barking Broadway and sat waiting. At ten thirty he saw the lights dim a couple of times and about fifteen minutes later gaggles of people started to congregate on the street, smoking and waving each other off into the night. He saw Alfie with his arms around a girl in a group of five, the others all being big navvy looking fuckers, her brothers he guessed. The girl was pretty, really nice looking, red hair piled up loosely on her head as she hoisted her short white mac, covering their two heads against the rain. Danby climbed out of the Daimler and called out to Alfie. The boy hesitated, spoke to Sophie briefly, then he trotted over to the car while the others sheltered in a doorway, the girl staring unblinking at Danby, looking fierce.

"Alright son?"

"Yeah, alright Mister Danby. What's occurring?"

"He wants to see you."

Alfie looked over at Sophie. She beckoned him over urgently. One of the louts called out to hurry up. Alfie shushed them with a gesture and turned back to Danby.

"Nah, fuck it Mister Danby, I'm out. I thought about what you said before and I had a chat with Declan over there. I'm going on the buildings, got a job up at the airport, I can start next Monday, so - well, sorry and all that but he can whistle."

"What about the flat? Son now listen, there'll be consequences."

"You said –"

"Yeah, I know what I said."

"If I don't do it now I might never, you know how he is, well – I'm not sure you do actually, but anyway, I mean it."

Two of Sophie's brothers sauntered over and stood alongside Alfie. They were big brutes, dressed up in suits and white shirts, but to Danby they were just Irish spud eaters out of the bog, and he paid them no mind.

"Alright there boy?" said one, addressing Alfie, "time to roll, getting wet as an Otter's pocket over there." Danby opened the passenger door and spoke quietly to Alfie. "Get in – we can talk on the way." Alfie shook his head, turned and walked back towards Sophie. He spoke over his shoulder.

"I'm done Mister Danby, sorry to lumber you mate, so long."

"Time to houl yer whisht there, big man. Now, off you go and stay well away, alright?"

Danby looked the man straight in his face and smiled.

"What now?" The man said, looking ready for it. Danby turned and got into the car. He started the engine and moved off slowly, heading back into the city and on to Islington. In his rear view he watched the men swagger back to the young couple, until the rain clouded the back window obscuring his vision. He could have taken them, he was sure. But in truth, he was pleased that Alfie was out of the racket. He drove through the rain to his flat, and waited for the phone call that he knew must be coming.

# Chapter Eight

Despite the fact of his day off, Rake had woken at dawn, and he spent the next hour or so noticing the numerous physical and psychological irritations that haunted his nights. His feet itched, he had a headache and his bowels were knotted and aflame. He decided to go to work. As soon as he got into his office Henrietta entered with coffee and a couple of biscuits. She didn't mention his unscheduled arrival. Rake dipped a biscuit into the cup; it broke off, half of it floating miserably in the liquid. Carefully he spooned it out and ate it.

"Like a rusk," he said, dunking the remaining half and eating it. "Nice."

"His lordship requests an audience, at the double." Rake groaned and wiped a hand across his face. The Chief Super was a pain, all bosses were a pain, and he always felt that Harper could see right through him. It was just the man's assumption that everyone was guilty of something, and Rake always felt guilty anyway, so it was excruciating, especially as this time there were tangible deceits being played out. Rake exhaled and dragged his weary bones from his chair.

"If I'm not back in thirty minutes ring through and say there's an emergency. Mind you, if I'm not back in thirty minutes I'll have strangled him, so there will be a ruddy emergency." He walked up the stairs to the second floor and into the small reception. He nodded to Harper's assistant who ushered him into the office with a nod. Harper was reading a file, or maybe pretending to, making him wait standing. Then, without looking up, he signalled for Rake to take a seat. The silence continued as Harper shuffled papers. Finally he looked up.

"So, fill me in." Rake thought about the double meaning and smiled. "What?" Harper enquired.

"Which case?"

"Start with the Frazer murder."

"It's all in that report, sir," Rake said, pointing at the file. "I think that the suicide of the boy Huff followed on from some sort of homosexual tryst, maybe a rape, in Tangier last November. I think that Frazer helped set up the connection, maybe to pay off a debt, I haven't established that yet, but it seems likely. My best guess is that one of Huff's friends cottoned on and murdered Frazer. Did a pretty good job of covering the murder up by torching the flat, but the second post mortem rectified that, and here we are."

"Suspects?"

"Like I said, the cohort of Huff's friends, primarily. The papers here didn't push the sexual angle, though some foreign papers did go into more detail, but Frazer's name wasn't mentioned in connection with the boy's suicide. So it's narrowed down to those in the know."

"Who had sex with the lad?"

"We're closing in on that. Haven't got a name yet, but I've got a description, and a connection with a face called Danby. It won't be long."

"You hope."

"No, I know."

"Your famous gut instinct?"

"Legwork, sir."

"What about Danby?"

"I'm working on it."

Harper nodded and shuffled the papers once more. He slid a piece of paper from under the folder and scanned it thoughtfully.

"How's the drinking?"

Rake's jaw muscles clenched and his cheek pulsed involuntarily. He pushed a digit onto the muscle and leaned the supporting elbow onto the arm of the chair.

"I don't know what you're getting at, sir."

Harper looked at the piece of paper, holding it up slightly at an angle.

"D.S. Sweet has asked for a transfer."

"I recommended it. He'd be better off at Vice, or maybe a move to robbery, something at the Yard."

"Not from the Department, Rake, just from working with you. He states," Harper was reading, " that you are inconsistent, irascible and bullying toward him and that you are collusive in your attitude to suspects during interview. He also claims that you smell of drink and that your methods are," he flicked his eyes over the paper, "inscrutable".

Rake's hand started to tremble and he hooked his thumb under his chin to steady it. He exhaled through his nose; this was anger now, not nerves.

"Is that a formal complaint, sir?"

"It's a request for a transfer, Rake."

"I'm not everyone's cup of tea. I wish he'd said something to my face, but I'm not too fussed to be honest."

"He states that you were assaulted by a suspect," he scanned the paper again, "Maurice Cohen, and that you refused to make a charge. That you harangued him – Sweet that is - for demonstrating a natural concern about a pederast and that you assaulted a member of the public without making a report."

"That's all out of context."

"Really, is it?"

"It's bollocks, sir."

"Mind your tongue in here Rake, this isn't the canteen."

"Sorry sir, that was uncalled for."

Harper breathed heavily and sat back in his chair. The two men looked at one another, then Harper stood up and walked around his desk, perching on the corner and looking down at Rake. He took a pack of cigarettes from his pocket and offered one to Rake, who raised a hand and shook his head. Harper struck a match and lit his cigarette, flicking the spent match into the empty grate.

"Look, you're a good copper, I know that. But honestly, I'm beginning to think it's you who needs a transfer, maybe the Flying Squad would be more your cup of tea, I could put in a word."

"Anything you say sir, so long as I can finish the cases I'm working on."

"Then you need to work it out with D.S. Sweet, I've denied his request. To be honest Rake, I think he's been promoted above his ability. He was better off in uniform." Harper stood and walked to the door. He opened it a tad then turned back to Rake. "But you need to watch it, sharpen up, he's got his eye on you." He opened the door fully and saw Rake out. "And so have I. Don't give him any more ammunition, lad." Rake nodded and headed back to the stairs. Harper was a wily old bird. Rake knew that he was being kept with Sweet in an effort to keep him in line, but in truth, he appreciated and was surprised by the old man's support, however qualified. On the way to his office he passed by Sweet's desk. The Sergeant's eyes flicked up to meet Rake's when he felt his presence, but he averted them as soon as he saw whom it was.

"Get a car. We'll visit Chuck Blizzard or Johnny Rocket, phone and see if one of them is at home."

Sweet was flooded with relief; he'd expected the worst. He didn't really know Rake well enough to know that the worst was coming, it was inevitable, and it just needed to come at a time when it could be savoured.

Danby parked the Daimler outside Deeming's apartment building. His phone had rung into the early hours; he'd let it ring. His eyes felt heavy and his neck ached with tension. Sixteen years: like a marriage stranded in the doldrums they were tired of one another - dog-tired. Not only was Deeming acting like a man possessed – the blackmail nonsense and Alfie Atkins, but also the chaps were moving in like a pack of wolves. Without him, Danby, there to oversee the various operations - the toms, the racetracks, the protection, the long firms and the gambling, let alone the clubs – the lads were shuffling to fill the vacuum. Plus the other firms, the Maltese, the Italians and the blacks in Notting Hill! He was out of touch. But he could sense that things were shifting. He wanted out.

He had eyed up a pub on Canvey Island, where he'd been raised, and where he had the only proper mates he'd ever known. He was coming up on forty-two, time to pull the plug. Pull the plug before his muscles got soft and his chain smoking turned his lungs into crispy bacon. Pull the plug before Deeming cut him adrift, had him floating in the Thames naked, wrapped in chicken wire, like they'd done to Sweeney, what, only two years ago, when he'd talked about going back to Glasgow and his family. Naked in the Thames, sunken in that murky soup, without his hands, without his head – fed to the pigs on that

84

Suffolk farm up by Lavenham. And Deeming, he'd lost the plot, totally. So many unforced errors, all because he couldn't keep his cock in his pants or his emotions in check. He'd been like a totem for Danby, the toughest nut in the West End. So what if he was a pouf, so fucking what? He steamed in like Tommy Farr when necessary, sorted them all out, but up against the twins – now? Or Mad Frankie and Billy Hill? Deeming with his bald patch and fat gut? Do me a favour! He'd stick with Chelsea, even though they were shit, that was a given, but Deeming? Now that was a long shot.

He snapped out of his reverie and walked round to the front of the block. He'd decided not to use his key. He pressed the buzzer and the door clicked open, he was expected. He walked up to the flat and rang the bell. The girl, Carmen, let him in wordlessly and scurried off somewhere. She looked like she'd had a bad morning, hair all mussed and clothing disassembled, poor little cow. Danby shrugged off his coat and laid it over the back of a chair, and then he walked, without knocking, into the master suite. Deeming was sitting up in bed with a breakfast tray resting across his lap. He spooned some soft-boiled egg onto a piece of toast and chewed. He nodded towards the chaise and Danby sat, lighting a cigarette.

"Tea, coffee?" Deeming offered.

"You're alright."

Deeming nodded and continued with his breakfast. He made it last a long time. Eventually he rang the little tinkling bell that sat on his bedside cabinet. Carmen entered shiftily, like a scolded puppy, and removed the tray. She asked if he needed anything else, or Mister Danby? Nothing – so she departed as silently as she'd entered. Deeming lit a cigarette and they both smoked in silence. The room felt to Danby like a sauna, even though it was so cold outside. He resisted the urge to remove his jacket - he had to.

"Your phone busted?" Deeming asked after a while.

"No – I was out, wasn't I? Looking for Alfie, didn't find him".

"Didn't you? And there you were, out all night, looking. You must have got soaked. It was plothering all night, fuck me, surprised you didn't catch a chill, what with all that rain."

"Yeah, well – I'm fine."

"That's a result."

They sat in silence, Deeming sipping at his tea, smoking his cigarette.

"I'll head off then. Got a lot to catch up on, just thought I'd check in."

"No, you're alright, you hang on for a while. Bring me up to speed, eh? So then, where was it you went looking?"

"Everywhere."

"But like where exactly? What, Ilford, the flat?"

"Yes, the flat."

"Where else, Barking?"

"Yes."

"You went to Barking, to the slag's house?"

"Yes."

"That it?"

"I drove about."

"What, all night, driving about in the Daimler were you?"

"Yes."

"Popping in and out, chapping on doors?"

"That's right."

"Did you search inside the various properties, or were you taking no for an answer?"

"I had a look."

"What, under beds, in wardrobes?"

"He wasn't about."

The buzzer sounded. They heard Carmen speak briefly on the entry phone. Danby looked over at the bedroom door. They waited now in silence. Shortly the doorbell rang. They heard Carmen answer that she was coming. The door opened and closed. There were voices, brief and subdued. Danby stood and collected himself. Deeming swung his legs out of the bed and pulled his dressing gown more tightly about his bulk.

"Sit down," he commanded.

"You've got company."

"Sit down, they're here to see you."
The bedroom door opened and Alfie tripped awkwardly into the room, followed by Danieli and Brumfitt, looking well pleased with themselves. Alfie's face was bruised and he had a cut lip.

"What's this?" Deeming seethed, " I never said to duff him up. Come here boy, come on." Deeming opened his arms to Alfie. The boy looked toward Danby, confused and distressed, but he stood his ground. Deeming dropped his arms to his side. He sat back down on the bed. Then he turned to Danby.

"You lied to me. They found him at the polony's. He says you saw him in Barking, right? You saw him and the slag out on a razzle, right? And you just let him go. What's the matter with you?

"What's the matter with me?" Danby suddenly roared, "what's the matter with me? Jesus, what's the matter with *you*? Do these two mutt's know what you've had me doing last couple of weeks? Nursing this poor twerp and trying to track down John Deakin because he's got the skinny on you tupping some other little boy. You're a fucking joke, mate; I'm out and so is Alfie." He stabbed his finger at Deeming, "try and stop me, you lousy pouf." He dropped his left arm down and the iron bar slid into his palm. He tore it hard across Danieli's jaw and the thug dropped like a sack of spuds. Brumfitt took a step back, fumbling inside his coat for a weapon, but Danby was upon him, bringing the bar down viciously on the crown of his head. Brumfitt made a low bellowing sound on an exhaling breath and collapsed. Danby hit him again, twice, just to make it harder for Deeming. He looked over at his boss, breathless but exultant. He pointed the bar at him and gritted: "You want some?" Deeming reached suddenly, desperately, towards his pillow, but Danby was quicker. He hoisted the bar up and snapped it down on Deeming's arm.

"Fuck that," Danby said. He flung the pillow to one side and brought up the Webley Mark IV that he knew was kept there.

Deeming nursed the injured arm, but he didn't cry out, he just blanched, his eyes watering, his lips purple, his breathing laboured. Danby began to steer Alfie towards the door, the boy struggling to take it all in as he stepped over the recumbent Brumfitt.

"How far do you think you'll get, boy?" Deeming said. Danby levelled the revolver at him, cocking the hammer.

"Shut your mouth," he said evenly. He pushed the boy through the door. Carmen was standing in the hallway. She watched them approach, eyes wide, focused on the gun. Danby stuck the revolver into his waistband and pulled out his note clip. He peeled off five pounds or thereabouts and pressed it into her palm.

"I were you sweetheart, I'd make myself scarce."
She nodded dumbly and headed off to get her coat. Danby took Alfie out and down into the car park. He bundled him into the Daimler and executed a fine three-point turn. As they pulled onto the street he experienced a moment of pure elation, until he became aware that he was purposefully holding back on the fear. And then, of course, the very act of noticing heralded its flooding arrival.

Charlie Goole lived in a nice little terraced house on the outskirts of Maida Vale. He seemed to be more affluent than Gupta, Cohen and Muir, so Rake guessed that Chuck Blizzard must have worked out okay for him. Goole was a good looking man of twenty three, tall, slim – his coiffure dyed blonde, almost white, his face chiselled, with cheekbones so sharp they could cut you. He wore a white shirt, a knitted tie and a loose cardigan. His slacks were tight fitting, a sort of shot silk, silver in a colour that matched his hair. His ice blue eyes were intelligent, and he held Rake's with an easy confidence, not challenging exactly, but almost. They'd gone through the usual rigmarole, Sweet sitting on the armchair and Goole on the sofa, with Rake on a dining chair pulled from an adjacent room.

"I have to say," Rake said looking about the room, "you seem to be doing alright, I mean compared to Elmo and Deacon for example, quite a contrast in fact. "

"I do okay. I've been in the game a bit longer," he shrugged and leaned an arm over the back of the sofa. "Started off on television, bit of a child star, I was the son in that programme with Alfie Bass, then I was in the theatre, you remember Meet me on the Corner? No, well anyway, and I made a few investments, Logan sort of guided me, property mostly. I've managed to put a bit away. Being a teen idol is a short-term thing, obviously. I planned ahead."

"So, Logan mentored you then? Like with Roy Huff, you were a special project."

"Roy was a special project," Rake noticed the bristle, "I was an investment. It's different."

"Different how?"

Goole leaned forward, his forearms trapped beneath his knees, his palms pressed together. Rake thought to himself: he's going to pontificate; he knew he would, twerp.

"Logan could see that I was a talent, I mean, I had form – what with the television, the stage, I was basically an actor who could sing, I've got my equity card," he looked at both policemen. "I've done legit theatre, you know – in the provinces, earned my stripes. So he saw me in West Side Story at Her Majesties a couple of years back and signed me. I still act, you'll have seen me in Dixon of Dock Green only last, when was it...?"

"No, I didn't see it."

"You're pulling my leg", he gave a short sharp laugh. "Busman's holiday I suppose."

"I don't have a box," said Rake.

"I saw it," Sweet said. "You played a pop singer."

"That's right."

"Not really acting then, was it."

Goole didn't know how to respond he deflated, just a little. For once Sweet's hostility had proved timely. Goole was a soufflé, a windbag – and they were getting nearer to the core of the man. Rake signalled Sweet to pull back.

"How did you feel when you found out Frazer was murdered?"

"How do you think I felt?"

"Depends."

"Depends on what?"

"On who inherits? Huff is dead; you seem to be his other golden boy. What do you think? He had no family, no wife, no

kiddies, some cousins up in Aberdeen he hasn't seen for years. There is a will, we know that, you might be on for a few bob."
    Goole started fiddling with his ring, it looked to Rake like white gold with a small sapphire surrounded by diamonds, jazzy.
    "I wasn't his golden boy."
    "That was Huff then, what – nose put out of joint?"
    "I'm not bent, if that's what you're inferring. Look, I reckon I need my brief, I think you're questions are hostile. If I'm a suspect say so, just don't fanny about."
    "So how did you feel, about Frazer I mean?"
    "How would you feel if your boss was murdered?"
Sweet laughed out loud, Rake didn't crack a smile, but he did nod an acknowledgment.

Danby pulled up outside the Alfie's flat on Belmont Road and looked up and down the quiet street. He hadn't noticed any familiar motors on the journey, or parked along the thoroughfare. He hoped that Deeming was preoccupied dealing with Danieli and Brumfitt, but he wasn't taking any chances. He palmed the Webley and opened the door.
    "Wait here."
He climbed out and walked up the path that led to the door of the upstairs flat. He rang the bell and stood back and to the side. He heard the sound of feet descending the stairs and ratcheted the hammer, keeping the gun by his side. The door opened and Alfie's mum, Joan, stuck her head out and looked around, starting momentarily when she saw him.
    "Oh, hello Mister Danby, " she craned her neck towards the street, "you looking for Alfie boy? He's not here, didn't come home – is that him in the car?"
    "Anyone up there with you?"
    "No, what do you mean?"
Danby signalled to Alfie, the boy got out of the car and trotted up the path. Joan Atkins put her hand to her mouth and took a step forward to meet him. She held his shoulders and looked at his face, then at Danby.
    "What's this, Mister Danby, what's happened?"

"It's alright ma," said the boy. "You need to go and get your coat on, and some shoes, and get the money out of the tin, we're in a hurry." She let go of Alfie and turned again to face Danby.

"What's going on? What's this all about, who done it?" Danby spun her gently back inside the door and guided Alfie in after her.

"Get going sweetheart, I'll explain in the car. Some naughty boys are coming, and they'll not be long." He closed the door as they went upstairs. He looked at his watch. Then he walked back down to the street and sat on the low wall by the motor. He lit a cigarette. He watched the road. A couple of cars went by, then another travelling in the other direction. Then he saw the Humber, he recognised it. It was red and it was flash and he knew who was driving it. It pulled up parallel to the Daimler. The driver's window rolled down. Danby stood, walked over to the car and leaned down, his right arm resting on the roof, the left hand holding the Webley in his coat pocket.

"Hello ducks," said Billy Manuel, in his broad northern brogue. "You look peggerd, been a long day already, has it?"

"Been a long life, Billy," he looked down past Manuel. Barker was sitting in the passenger seat, a sawn off shotgun resting across his lap. He swivelled his eyes to the back where a fat bloke who he didn't recognise was sitting, leaning forward. The fat bloke was giving him daggers.

"Who you got back there Bill, Tubby Muffin?"

"That's Henry. Say hello to Mister Danby, Henry, no? No – well ducks, he's one of the strong silent types. Shite at parties."

"So – what's the game then, Bill? We having a proper showdown? High Noon, is it?"

"We're just here for the boy, that's all. Got a phone call, got me out of the sack, actually. I was with right nice lass too. Sixteen, she is, bangs like a shit house door in a hurricane."

"Yeah well, you do look a bit peaky, better get back to her then, I reckon."

"She'll wait."

"You sure?"

"I am," said Billy Manuel. "I tied the bitch up."

Suddenly Danby reached in and snatched the keys from the ignition flinging them onto the path, and then he took a step back, slid the iron bar into his right hand and poked it hard into Manuel's face. The Webley was in his left hand and he swung it left and right at Barker and the fat bloke.

"You," he said to Barker, "put your hands on the dash, now! You, you fat cunt, get out," he ratcheted the hammer. "Out!" He looked quickly up and down the street; it was quiet, for the moment. Alfie and his mum were coming out of the house.

"Get the keys," he said to Alfie. The boy collected the keys and put the woman into the back of the Daimler. "Come over here son, and get the sawn off, it's here, Barker's got it. Move yourself" Alfie jogged to the Humber and opened the passenger door, taking up the shotgun.

"Now, shoot the bastard." Alfie's eyes widened. Barker yelped, spun round and covered his face. Danby winked at the boy and indicated for him to get in the Daimler. He levelled the Webley at the big lad, who was standing now, almost in the middle of the road, caught between the desire to run and his fear as to what Manuel would do if he did. "You, lard arse, what's your name again?"

"Henry Oswell."

"Henry, alright Henry Oswell, take your coat off and drop it. Now your jacket."

Manuel was groaning, holding his blooded face, crimson spreading darkly through his fingers. He was saying something, but it was incomprehensible to Danby, the adrenaline blocking the words, though every other sense was heightened. Oswell's jacket landed heavily, his gun, Danby thought, all right – time to go. The whole mess had taken no more than two minutes, but someone might be on the phone to the police. He climbed into the Daimler and they tore up Belmont Road heading towards Goodmayes. Joan Atkins babbled all the way, Alfie trying to smooth her out, Danby saying nothing at all. Danby parked near the station and turned to face them. He handed Alfie all the money he had on him, thirty quid, maybe a bit more.

"You two need to disappear. Get a train and go, somewhere, a relative or something that *he* doesn't know about."

"But what about Sophie?" Alfie said.

"Phone her, but don't tell her where you are. I mean it, but she needs to get lost too, he'll be after her, no doubt about it, mate. You need to take care of your mum. He'll have her teeth out, her nails, come on – you know the score. Get going." Alfie steered his mum from the car, she looked fifteen years older already, and he didn't envy the boy. Not one bit. Alfie leaned back and spoke through the window, through the teeming rain, through his fear.

"I don't know what to do, Mister Danby."

Danby put the big motor into gear and pulled sharply away from the kerb. Same here, son, he thought to himself. Isn't it a bastard?

# Chapter Nine

Rake walked from the office into Soho and stepped gratefully out of the rain. The Coach and Horses was quiet, just the usual barfly's in evidence, Jeffrey Bernard drinking with George Barker and Eddie Linden at the bar and a clique of journalists sitting at a corner table. Rake walked along the bar and went into the toilet. When he came out Bernard was sitting alone nursing a vodka. Rake ordered him a refill along with a large whiskey, which he drank off in a gulp. He hadn't sat down.

"Not staying?" Bernard enquired.

"Heading home, just taking the chill off. Have you heard from Deakin?" Bernard shook his head, and with a brief salute he took up his drink. Rake noticed that Norman Balon was hovering. Balon twitched his head and Rake followed him further along the bar.

"That ponce came in, the one I mentioned, you remember? The one looking for Deakin." Rake nodded and Norman leaned in conspiratorially. "He got a bit up himself, actually, but I saw him off."

"Yes, and?"

"He said he worked for Noel Deeming, said I was due a visit, actually."

"What do you mean?"

"He was being threatening, trying to put the mockers on me, I told him where to get off, fucking schmuck. Anyway, I thought you would want to know, so now you do."

"Right, yes – that's helpful Norman, no, it is. Strange though, that he'd put him up just like that." Norman Balon shrugged and walked along the bar to serve a customer. Rake walked back to the empty stool alongside Jeff Bernard.

"Two more," he said to Balon. The drinks were poured. "Describe the ponce again, Norman."

"Big, maybe six two, six three. He had a proper rabbit skin titfer, Camel hair coat with a velvet collar, neat – poncey, like I said." Rake nodded, they'd met outside a phone box in Camden: Danby. Rake patted his coat pocket, he'd forgotten about the knucks, but there they were still, nestling there like a sleeping mastiff. Bernard drank his vodka and stood, a little unsteadily.

"Better get back to Jackie, thanks for the drink, my turn next time round. Listen, if you do see Deakin – he owes me money, he did a photograph of me, promised me a drink. If you're interested put a score on Merriman II for the National, it's a cert." He ran his hand through his thick dark hair, tipped a "so long" to Balon and wended his way towards the Greek Street exit. The pub was beginning to fill, so Norman wandered off to serve. Rake sipped at his drink, thinking about Danby, and why he might be showing his hand regarding Noel Deeming. He'd never met Deeming, but of course he knew who he was. He knew about his reputation.

After the war, when Jack Spot and Billy Hill had ruled the London underworld, Deeming had been an also ran, but along with the twins and the Richardson's, he'd built a solid reputation for thuggery and violence, and taken over or set up nefarious enterprises in the western boroughs, and lately in the West End. When Spot and Hill fell out Deeming had consolidated his hold on spielers in Notting Hill, clubs in Soho and Mayfair and any other of the myriad and lucrative avenues for illicit money making throughout the city. He'd had a few pulls, but apart from a spell in the glasshouse towards the end of the war, he'd never been convicted. He'd follow it up in the morning. He took a whiskey mac and had a cigarette, then he said farewell to Norman Balon and took his leave.

Danby left the Daimler in Stratford and went to a Barclays, drawing out a hundred and sixty quid. Then he took the tube to Liverpool Street where he hopped on a train to Southend Central and thence by taxi to the Westcliff Hotel. He booked himself a room and ordered some sandwiches. Everything cash from now on, no cheques, no trail. He stood on the balcony and watched the tide coming in. The rain had ceased and a few couples were to be seen, catching the last light of the day. He sat on his bed and ate his sandwiches, and then he went down to the bar and had a couple of drinks. The late January freeze meant that the hotel was quiet, just a couple of salesmen types talking loudly, leaning against the counter, and a strange couple, the woman with a pronounced goitre, the man heavyset, his stomach protruding nakedly from his unbuttoned midriff, sitting on a sofa by the exit. Fucking depressing, Danby thought. He walked over to the bar. The barmaid was pretty, in a faded kind of way, but her mouth was drawn down and her uniform was dusty and stained, so Danby just ordered his drink and sat back down. Danby hadn't had sex for a couple of years, he'd tried it a few times after Rosemary left him, but it had been empty and dispiriting; a duo of whores who'd not had the money owing to Deeming. After that, he'd just handed over his own money when needed, and forgone the listless gratuity. I'm all heart, he thought to himself. He took another drink. The couple were still there, in the gloomiest part of the room. Both had nodded off, neither had bought a drink, although Danby noticed three empty crisp packets laying haphazardly on the table in front of them, salt from the blue twists spread over the laminate.

The rain came again with the dark. It pounded unhappily on the glass canopy above the reception area, echoing through the lobby and into the bar, roiling like the tide, carried on gusts of wind that rattled the door leading off to the terrace and the greensward beyond.

"Better call us a taxi," one of the salesmen said to the barmaid. "I don't fancy walking in this."

"You'd better tell them at reception, I don't order taxi's."

"Blimey girl – there's only us in here, won't take you a minute."

"I don't order taxi's."

"Righto," said the other salesman. They walked out of the bar muttering rudely about the hotel being a morgue. The barmaid seemed rather embarrassed, looking expectantly at Danby, so he walked back to the counter and ordered another double.

"You didn't need that," he said pleasantly.

"It takes all sorts," she huffed. He realised that she'd been enjoying the company, and that her petulance was simply disappointment at their pending departure. No good turn goes unpunished, he thought to himself, as he sat back down with his drink.

Rake lay on his bed fully dressed and let the night come in heavy. He didn't turn on his lamp or the radio or the fire. If someone had entered the room they might well have thought he was dead. But no one was coming, not tonight, he hoped. In his sleep he dreamed that someone was banging on a door, a long way off. The rhythmic beat began to get louder, it had a threatening edge - perhaps a giant was approaching: a Golem. He awoke with a start. It was the telephone. Rake grunted, shook his head to clear the muzz, and clicked on the bedside lamp. Picking up the receiver he glanced at the clock, it was only eleven fifteen.

"Rake," he said.
"Is this Cyril Rake?"
"Who's this?"
"My name is Caldwell, I'm Senior Registrar at the Maudsley Hospital. I have been asked to contact you by Ruth Campbell-Rake, she says that you are her husband."

Rake was sitting up now; he fumbled for a cigarette and struck a match on the latch of the suitcase. "What's happened?"

"Your wife took an overdose of phenobarbital on Tuesday night. Luckily she was found in time."

"Who found her?"

"A young man, he called the ambulance, probably saved her life. Anyway, she would like you to bring some clothing, nightgowns, underwear and a dressing gown, oh - and her makeup bag, you know the drill, I'm sure."

"So she's able to talk?"

"Yes, yes – certainly."

"I'd like to speak to her."

"She's asleep, I'm afraid you won't get any sense out of her tonight. Obviously it isn't the designated visiting time, but I'm sure you can spend a few minutes with her. Ask for me, Caldwell, when you arrive."

"Fine, I'll be there as soon as I can."

Rake went into his kitchen and splashed water on his face. Then he went out onto the Charing Cross Road and hailed a taxi to take him to Putney. Thankfully he still had a key to the house.  As he travelled past the inky river it dawned on Rake: she'd taken his tablets and tried to kill herself with them. He found it an effort to keep the word that was creeping into his consciousness at bay.

The Marylebone Yacht Club didn't live up to its name. Located under railway arches near Melcombe Place it was a notorious dive, infamous following a stabbing in 1958, where a Scot called Sweeney had been killed, this was the rumour anyway, being as the man had disappeared, the body never to be found. The licence was held by a chap called Landau, though in fact Noel Deeming owned the club. He had summoned the firm to attend a meeting there, on that stygian night, having had the place cleared before his midnight rendezvous. Danieli was there, though there was no Brumfitt, being as he was still in the hospital. Billy Manuel and Barker were in attendance too, although Henry Oswell seemed to have thought better of it. Kenny Hurren and Harry Coleman had been invited, primarily to make up the numbers. The only senior member of the team missing was Danby. And the one item on the agenda was of course, Danby. Deeming certainly wasn't going to bring up the matter of Deakin and the missing negatives, and Alfie could wait. He strode into the club having had Vernon drive him. Vernon had to wait in the car; he hadn't much time for Vernon. Deeming walked over to the card table, where the boys were sitting, bunched around one end, as if waiting to be auditioned, or to audition Deeming, who had been so neglectful since Christmas. Deeming shook the rain from his overcoat as he slipped it off and hung it on the back of his chair. He sat down heavily and told Hurren to fetch him a bottle of Scotch.
	"Top all these cunts up."
Hurren went round filling glasses, then filled Deeming's glass, laying the bottle carefully within his reach.
	"Health gentlemen," Deeming said, raising his glass. "I noticed that you all got a bit quiet when I came in. What have I missed?" No one said anything in reply; in fact they didn't even look at one another. So there they sat in silence, Deeming letting

it build, enjoying their discomfiture. "What then?" he said after a while "let me guess. You were talking about our dear old pal Danby, what's gone Tonto, gone off the fucking reservation, right? Am I right? So come on, what's the gossip?" This was when they started to look at each other, and then Danieli tipped his chair back on its hind legs and spoke up.

"It isn't gossip, boss, is it? I mean, when me and B. turned up at your gaff we were a bit taken aback by the reception Mister Danby gave us, right? We weren't expecting a biffing, and then, what with him kicking off at Billy and that," his chair cracked down onto four legs, the smack echoing around the room like a gunshot. "Bit of a choker, all things considered." Manuel spoke up at this point, having considered his options he opted for a forthright expression of feeling.

"Cunt broke my fucking nose. I see him again I'm going to fucking shoot him."

"That's not going to happen, Bill. No – you see him you bring him to me. But the priority in this particular interval is the taking care of business, you've let things slip, you've been slipshod, not all your fault, not by a long shot, it's Danby been letting things slide, I know that, we all know that, don't we? Of course we do."

The door at the back of the club shut with a ringing clang, all heads turned and looked towards the bar and the door that led off to the car park. They heard footsteps approaching along the corridor. Then the inner door opened and a silhouette, backlit by the lights of the outer hallway, entered the room. He stood back. He went to the optics, took up a stubby glass and filled it with Scotch. He turned, sniffed the drink and looked up.

"Most of you know Lenny Matta," Deeming purred. "He's here for Danby."

The clique just stared, first at Lenny Matta, then at Deeming.

"Look boss," Danieli said, "I don't know what's occurring between you and Mister Danby, but if you want a meet I'll sort it. We don't need his sort getting involved, no offence Lenny," he nodded over at Matta. "This is personal, internal housekeeping, no need to contract out."

"Oh is that right?" Deeming said. "Well Danby went through you cunts like a dose of salts. Anyway, Lenny's in, that's an executive fucking decision, so shut your cake hole and listen. There's one job for you Dano, you and me is going to visit H.H. Bender tonight. Then it's off to work you go, our dinner's don't cook themselves, as my dear old mum used to say, know what I mean? You lot sit and have a chinwag with Lenny here and give him everything you got on where he might find Mister Danby. You Dano," he indicated Danieli "come with me."

Deeming stood, dragging his coat from the chair and draping it over his broad shoulders as he headed for the door. Danieli looked at his familiars and over at Matta, scowling. Then he stood and followed Deeming into the howling night.

Rake sat on an orange plastic chair at the bedside of his insensate wife, haloed in the subtle glow of the single bulb that flickered, humming, above her bed. Caldwell had ushered him into the room, and he didn't feel that he could leave until the requisite time had passed, though he had no idea how long that should be. Ruth looked beatific in her stillness; the strain had left her brow and her cheeks seemed fuller than usual, her flesh smooth and flushed pink in the still heat of the room. Rake spoke in a low, resonant voice:

"Do you remember, that time in October fifty eight, after the riots – I was called out to that house in Notting Hill? That woman, Negro woman, up on the ledge, her flat had been gutted by fire – remember? Her baby had died, smoke inhalation, anyway, so she's five floors up on the ledge of this tenement and she's going to jump. I got the call and I'm standing there on this ledge and there's a mighty gale blowing and there we are, standing maybe three feet apart, and she means it, she's serious, she's about to go, and I'm standing alongside her and I don't know what to say. What I do know, is I know I've got to say something – but I can't say the wrong thing, right? And I've got to do something, but I can't do the wrong thing or she'll go, and I know she *will* jump. And there's this whipping wind battering me and I'm terrified. My fingers are grappling for some kind of purchase, but there's nothing, just brickwork and I'm looking down and I'm looking up and I'm looking at her and I don't know what to do. Then my mouth get's frozen, it's like I've got lockjaw, and my whole face is a rictus. " Rake looked at his hands as they rested on his lap. Then he looked at Ruth as tears sprang unbidden into his eyes.

"That was our marriage, sweetheart, in the end. I'm sorry, I'm truly sorry. But you see, she jumped, or rather she just let herself go limp and she leant into the wind and fell, swooping briefly – it seemed, then she plummeted. The crowd parted like a wave. I watched her all the way down. And for a moment there I leant into the wind too. I was going to follow her down. It was an instinct, I don't know where it came from or why it came, it just did. And, see, I know that you were taking me down, so I left you. I'm not coming back. I can't cope with the hysteria." He stood and watched over her for a moment, then he turned and walked out of the room, past Caldwell, past the nurses station and away. He didn't look back.

Deeming instructed Vernon to slow down to a crawl as they got to Sandhurst Road in Catford. They cruised past the spieler and pulled into the kerb twenty or so yards further along the street, away from the lights. Vernon switched the engine off and they sat, the three of them, waiting. Deeming had had a tip that H.H. Bender was due in for a game of poker in the private back room. It was time to make an example, to shore up his authority, put a bit of stick about, and H.H. was an outstanding issue, due for one – definitely. He looked at his watch; it was ten past one. The Magnette wasn't as comfortable as the Daimler, and it was a bit of a squeeze in the back, so Deeming told Danieli to move into the front. But as Dano climbed out he saw Bender coming from the spieler, and Bender saw Danieli, or at any rate he saw a big figure and a motor with bodies in it, illuminated by the courtesy lights, and he flew off in the other direction. Danilei jumped back onto the rear seat and Vernon made a U turn, caroming off the side of a stationary vehicle on the other side of the road before speeding up Sandhurst towards the Church Hall. They saw Bender at last, his mac billowing under streetlights as he ran limping along the pavement. Deeming was laughing, a throaty hiccough, ugly – it unsettled Vernon, who hadn't been briefed and didn't know what was happening. Bender swung into a narrow alleyway and the car screeched to a halt.

"Fetch him back," Deeming ordered, still vaguely amused. Danieli and Vernon flew out of the Magnette and ran into darkness. They returned a couple of minutes later dragging Bender between them. Danieli pushed him in besides Deeming and he and Vernon climbed into the front of the car. They set off towards Eltham.

"Oh," Bender said when he saw it was Deeming.

"Oh? Is that it?" Deeming said.

"I thought we had it sorted, Mister Deeming. You got the photos; did you get the negatives off of Deakin? If not, I can fix that no problem. You want to tax me you can tax me, sure, if you'd said."

Danieli glanced sideways at Vernon, neither man had a clue as to what was afoot and it felt uncomfortable, being in the dark.

"Vernon, head down to Blackheath, the Golf Club." Vernon nodded and swung a right, heading down Court Road.

"What's occurring Mister Deeming? Look if you've still got a beef with me let me put it right. Here," he reached into his coat pocket and pulled out a roll of notes, "I done good tonight, got a Pony here, down payment."

"Put it away, you prat."

Bender thrust the money onto Deeming's lap and pulled his hand away as if it had been burned. Deeming brushed the notes onto the floor of the car, as he might the ash from a cigar. He looked out of the window, ignoring Bender, who just wouldn't shut up. It only took five minutes to get to the Golf Club. Deeming had planned to take Bender to Epping Forest, but he couldn't have put up with the man stinking up the car for an hour, so he'd improvise. He could improvise, why not? Deeming got out of the car and Vernon and Danieli got out too. But H.H. Bender sat looking bewildered, not moving anything except his head, which swivelled like an owl. Deeming signalled for his underlings to produce the man, and they started to drag Bender from the car. He kicked out screaming, like a maladjusted toddler being taken from a birthday party before time. Danieli looked up at Deeming.

Deeming gave a brief nod and Dano hit the man full on in the face. He went limp. They pulled him from the car.

Rake entered his room and propped a chair up against the door to keep it closed. He'd have to get a couple of padlock sets, good ones, when he had the time. He turned on the lights and the electric heater and flopped onto his bed. The phone began to ring. He thought immediately of the hospital, but it was Deakin, calling from a kiosk.

"Where are you? What happened?"

"I'm in Brighton, but I've run out of favours. I need money. Is it all right? I need to get back to London."

"No it isn't bloody all right, what do you mean is it all right, are you insane?"

"I don't know, what do you think?"

"I think you'd better start telling me the truth, you've been lying through your teeth since this all started."

"Can you wire me some money? Just enough to get me back to the smoke, Barclays, North Street, tomorrow."

"You can't stay here. What happened in my flat, was it Danby?"

"You have been busy."

"And what about Deeming? How is he involved?" There was a brief silence down the line. Then Deakin was back.

"I'll explain when I see you."

"You'll have to come in to the station, you can't stay here, and I mean it." The pips went, Deakin talked urgently, shouting over Rake's protestations.

"Barclays, North Street – tomorrow!" The line went dead. Rake hung up and went back to sit on his bed. He watched the phone for twenty minutes, but it didn't ring.

Deeming walked to the bunker on the eighth hole and looked down. The sand was as wet as if the tide had just gone out. The quartet just stood looking down, as if they were in this together, whatever this turned out to be. There was a momentary camaraderie, there in the moonlight, in the chill wet hours of that fragmentary morning. The spell was broken when Deeming kicked his foot into the back of Bender's knee. The little man collapsed, kneeling suddenly on the damp grass, as if in prayer. His mouth was moving silently, perhaps he *was* praying – if not now, Deeming thought, when? He pulled an old single bevel meat knife from inside his voluminous coat and handed it to Vernon.

"Off you go Vernon," he said. "No point dragging it out." Vernon shook his head, backing away a few stumbling steps. "No, not interested? Milky cunt. Come on then Dano, get stuck in." He handed the knife to Danieli. Bender fell onto his hands and knees and began crawling down into the bunker. He was making noise now, guttural barking yaps. He sounded to Deeming like an angry beggar, both bitter and pleading, it tickled him no end. He walked slowly, confidently towards the man and put his foot onto his back, flattening him in the sand. Deeming held his hand out towards Danieli, who handed him the knife blade first. Deeming flipped the blade and caught the handle expertly. Then he looked both Vernon and Danieli in the eye, each in turn.

"You don't need to watch, if it upsets you," he said. But neither man could turn away, they were mesmerised, or perhaps petrified, as still as marble in the moonlight. Deeming went down on his knees, hard, knocking the wind out of the struggling supplicant. He began to stab, to cut and to hack. It was butchery, pure and unhurried, clinical almost, at least in the beginning. Vernon vomited, predictably. Deeming didn't notice; he was preoccupied. Danieli lit a cigarette, nodding, at one point he said, "yeah, yeah." and tried a smirk – but it wouldn't have fooled anyone, if anyone had been looking. Finally Deeming stood up from the body. He staggered a little, breathless, in a post coital fugue, almost – or so it seemed to Vernon, who had previous with the big man.

"And that's that," he wheezed.

"Got a shovel in the car, boss?" Danieli asked, feigning some macho nonchalance.

"What, you want to bury him, here?"

"Whatever, you know?"

"Not a golfer then, Dano? Only about a foot of sand here, fucking moron, get rid of this," he tossed the knife onto the grass. "And do it proper, Vernon, drive me home. Here," he held out his hand and Vernon helped him onto the fairway, "we'll have a bit of breakfast, eh son? "

"What about him?" Danieli ventured.

"Leave it where it is, Dano. That's half the point."

Danieli didn't ask about the other half of the point. Something about photographs, about negatives, about someone called Deakin. It wasn't his place to enquire, so he collected the knife and watched Deeming and Vernon walk back towards the car park. He'd have to ring Billy Manuel, when he could find a kiosk, and get picked up. He took a last long look at H.H. Bender and began the long walk back to civilization.

# Chapter Ten

Danby had slept well. He stepped out onto the balcony of room 221 and smoked two cigarettes, enjoying the view over the greensward down towards the esplanade. To his left he could see the pier stretching out over the slate grey estuary. To his right he could make out the winding path that led towards the station and the fishing boats beyond. He felt at home, he was home, or nearly home. He took a shower, sponged his suit and got dressed. He'd have a wander up Hamlet Court Road and get a nice breakfast and then pop into a menswear shop and get kitted out proper. He couldn't face breakfast at the hotel, he'd had enough of the Westcliff.

    The rain had stopped and the early morning brought the sun. So when Danby walked down the steps of the hotel he crossed the road and took a path through the greensward heading down to the water. The whiff of petrichor there among the trees, the plants and the bracken was pleasing, and the salty spray from the wind-rippled water reminded him of a time before, of life on Canvey - of life, in fact. He nodded at the people promenading along the waterfront; and they nodded back in acknowledgement. He walked back up to Hamlet Court Road and had a fry-up and a big mug of tea. Then he went into Havens and bought a suit a shirt some underwear and a small leather suitcase. Finally he went into a kiosk and made his first phone call of the morning. First he rang Jimmy Watling in Basildon and got the loan of a motor. Then he rang Frank Hanley and arranged for him to slip back to the smoke to fetch his passport and the money he had stashed behind the bathroom cabinet. Finally he called his old mucker Basil Cumper at The Admiral Jellicoe on Canvey Island. He arranged for a room, just for a few days, nice and quiet – he knew the pub, and Basil was well pleased, couldn't wait to see him again, he said. It heartened Danby, hearing the warmth in his voice, old friends – all willing and able and true. Old friends, the old crew, still ready, still loyal – no questions asked, no price tags. He took a nice long walk, and then went back to the hotel to shower again and change his clothes. He'd said he'd meet Jimmy there to collect the motor, then off to drop him at his used car lot in Basildon, then the short drive over the bridge to Canvey. As he showered he thought: Am I a bad man capable of doing good things, or am I a good man capable of doing bad? Maybe, when I get to Spain, I'll have time to find out.

Alfie Atkins carried the breakfast tray up three flights of stairs to the bedroom he was sharing with his mother. She sat up in bed and he carefully laid the tray on her lap.

"Margaret says you've got to eat it all, she doesn't want a repeat performance, got it?" he said, scolding but solicitous. Joan nodded and picked up a slice of toast. Alfie walked to the window and looked down at the rooftops, stretching endlessly, it seemed, down towards the Mersey. He lit a cigarette and stood for some minutes, watching the rain. He didn't think he'd ever mentioned his auntie Maggie, or the boarding house or Liverpool, but there was always that nagging uncertainty. Deeming had never seemed interested in Alfie's life, his past – or his future, come to that. But he'd been so drunk; drunk enough that he could let the man fuss with him, he could have let it slip. He didn't think so, no, he didn't think so. He stubbed the cigarette out in a saucer and checked that Joan was still eating, and then he went downstairs to the phone and rang through to Sophie's house in Barking. Declan answered.

"Hello boy," he said, "what the fuck do you want?"

"Just wanted to make sure Sophie got off all right."

"Got off to where? 'Course she's not, she's here, but she won't want to talk with you, you fuckin' eejit."

"Declan, please – fetch her, I need to talk with her."

"Fetch her? She's not a fucking dog."

"But they'll come for her, to get to me. He'll come."

"You slippy fuckin' tit, why do you think I'm here? Let him come, now that's it, don't call again – and really, don't show your daft face or you'll know about it." The line went dead. Alfie stood for a moment, pondering. Then he replaced the receiver and walked slowly up the stairs to the bedroom. Joan had eaten most of the toast, but hadn't touched the boiled egg. Alfie sat at the foot of his bed and looked across at his mother. He felt as if he might cry. Perhaps he'd be better off alone, well of course, he would be. But she needed him - she seemed so helpless now. He hadn't realised how old she had become, only fifty-two, made prematurely old by his father, and now by him.

"Eat your egg," he said. He laid his head on the pillow and thought about Sophie, trying to stifle a dark and rising precognition.

"You all right, love?"

The question hung in the air like a heavy cloud, noxious and murky. He didn't know how to answer, and so he didn't. He could feel panic rising in his gut, like something unconscionable bursting from its pupa. He sat up and reached for his jacket.

"Auntie Margaret is down in the kitchen mum, it's nice and warm down there. Finish your breakfast, get dressed and go and spend some time with her, it'll be nice. But mum, please, remember – don't say anything about, well – you know."

"Tell her what, son? Say what exactly? I don't understand what's happened myself."

"Talk about the bloody weather then, mum."

She looked stung, her mouth fell open and tears welled in her rheumy eyes and then ran down her sunken cheeks. He pulled the jacket roughly from the chair back, and the heavy oak hit the floor with a crack. Margaret shouted from below, calling to see if all was well. Alfie dragged the jacket from the chair back as if he were taming it and left the room, taking the stairs two at a time and slamming through the front door and out into the rain, the clag and the street. Seagulls trekked with him on the long walk to the river. He sat on a wall looking at the brown lowering water, watching the ferry travel across towards Woodside, until it was lost to the fog. Reaching into his jacket pocket he counted the money he had left. He'd made his decision, or *a* decision anyway. He shuffled down from the wall and headed towards Lime Street. His mother would be all right with Auntie Maggie. He'd ring her, but right now he had to prioritize. One step at a time, focus on what's right, right for him. It was the only thing to do, and he was doing it.

Jimmy Watling turned up in a black Ford Consul saloon. Danby gave him a knuckle chuck under the chin and received a hard slap on the back in return. He looked over the motor, part amused and part disappointed.

"I was thinking of driving over to the Continent," he said.

"Don't worry about it, son – it'll go forever. Lovely piece of kit."

"I'm not a punter, Jimmy."

"No mate serious, stand on me."

They got into the car, Danby driving – and headed to the garage to drop Jimmy and get the bit of cash he was holding for a rainy day, the jalopy drove surprisingly well, it had obviously been tuned.

"What else do you need?" Jimmy asked as they drove through Hadleigh.

"Nothing, I've got it pretty much covered. I've got a room sorted for a couple of nights and Frank will grab me some stuff from the flat."

"Bit risky."

"He knows where I stash the spare keys, he'll go early dressed as a cozzer, he'll be all right."

"If you say so."

"Needs must, Jimmy."

"You got a tool?"

Danby nodded, thinking of the Webley, carried safely in the little suitcase.

"Lost my knucks though, shame eh? Had them since before the war. Sentimental value."

"Fuck me," Jimmy let out a guffaw. "I remember them since when we was tearaways down the Kursaal, pulling crumpet and having it with the East End cunts. Good times or what? Then you was gone up to the smoke, Mister Big Bollocks. Never should have gone, eh? Back now though. It's a left."

Danby pulled a sharp left and drew up at the garage. They got out and walked through the lot to the office. Jimmy sat at his desk and poured a couple of whiskeys. They saluted one another and lit up. Jimmy took a fat envelope from a drawer and tossed it to Danby.

"Got more than a ton in there, I bunged in a score for old times sake."

"Appreciated," Danby said, pocketing the envelope. They sat and smoked for a while in an easy silence. "All right, Jimmy. I'll head off. Once I get sorted I'll send you the money for the motor."

"I know you will, no hurry."

Danby left with no further words exchanged or needed. He drove south towards Canvey Island. He noticed the clouds that were bubbling up over the estuary, kept at bay by the brisk off shore wind, just gathering there like patient sentinels.

It was late when Rake got back to the Charing Cross Road. He'd stopped off at Shafi on Gerrard Street and eaten a lamb curry. It was repeating on him, spices and onion. As he walked up the alleyway a figure stepped lightly out of the shadows. Rake's hand instinctively gripped the brass knuckles as he stepped back crouching, but it was only Deakin.

"I told you to go to the station."

"You should have sent me the money then like you promised. I had to borrow the train fare off a friend, without asking him, not very nice after he'd put me up."

"Not my problem."

"I can't go to the station, can I? We need to get the story straight, Rakey, I don't want it to come out that you've been looking after me, shielding me, letting me bunk down with you."

Rake cuffed him hard round the ear. The little fellow howled and looked bewilderedly at Rake, like a little boy lost. Rake sighed and unlocked the door, leaving it open. Deakin followed him up the stairway and stood tentatively outside the room.

"You need to get that fixed," he said, tapping on Rake's door. After a few moments he pushed it fully open, standing there in the half-light, forlorn and uncertain. He watched as Rake took off his coat and clicked the fire into life. The policeman pulled out a chair and sat at the table, opening a bottle of Canadian Club and pouring two glasses.

"Everything," he said.

Deakin eased his way into the room. Keeping his coat on against the frigidity of the hollow room, he sat and gulped the whisky. He looked at Rake, and then looked down nodding, resigned.

"Tangier?" he said.

"Everything," Rake replied.

"Can I have a top up, please?"

Rake refilled the glass. Without another word, Deakin threw the liquor into Rake's face, and then he reached across the table and slapped him. Deakin stood, pushing his chair back with his legs and stepping towards the door. Rake blinked furiously as the whisky stung his eyes and dribbled from his chin. The shock subsided and he looked at Deakin in mild surprise. Then he burst out laughing.

"You snide little fucker!" Rake said, wiping his face with his handkerchief. "So that's how you did it, you crafty sod. Was it Danby?"

Deakin nodded. He was confused, alarmed, but still ready in case of retaliation. Rake poured whisky into Deakin's glass and waved him back into his seat.

"So what happened?"

"He got your address from David, he hurt him, though I didn't know that until later. He busted in and gave me a bit of stick, looking for the negatives. I told him they were in your suitcase, when he bent down to open it I hit him with the ashtray. I had to get away, so I took the train down to Brighton. Have you met Danby? He's a right evil bastard. I had no choice."

"Tell me about Tangier."

"Frazer invited me. He owed Noel Deeming a whole load of money, I don't know, I think Deeming had put up the backing on some scheme that went south. Anyway, Frazer set it up for Deeming to be with Roy Huff as part payment, or an act of goodwill or something. Frazer was in a bind, so he asked me to get some shots of Deeming in the act, which I did."

"For a consideration."

"Well not for fucking pleasure, you cunt!'

"Don't get your knickers in a twist, John."

"Well all right, fine, all right. But I didn't know the kid was going to top himself, it all got out of hand really quick. Frazer

111

was going to use the shots to put pressure on Deeming to back off, something to hold over the bastard. Then Frazer was killed, I didn't get paid, so I sold the photo's and kept the negs as security."

"Who bought the snaps?"

"Bender, H.H. – you'll know him."

"Who killed Frazer?"

"I don't know."

"All right, John – so who do you *think* killed Frazer?"

"At a guess it would be Danby, under orders. I didn't know it was murder until you told me. Put the frighteners on me."

"It's a mess, John, isn't it?"

"Yes it's a mess, it's a mess, but I didn't know all this was going to happen, did I? I didn't know the boy was unstable, not like that. Then the killing, it all went berserk, I didn't see any of it coming, how could I?"

"You colluded in a young boy, a child really, getting drugged and raped."

"I did, you're right, I fucking did, I did that. I colluded in a child getting raped. So what do I do now?"

"We go to the station tomorrow morning and you give a statement."

"What happens to me?"

"You go to jail."

"What happens to you?"

"I resign from the force."

"Can't I put it right?"

"There are two people dead, John. Neither of us can put it right."

They sat and continued drinking. The clock on Rake's bedside suitcase and the ticking of the electric fire were punctuated by the rattling of the window as wind gusted spasmodically down the Charing Cross Road. Then the rain came, tapping on the window like the nails of a restless hand drumming a tuneless percussive rhythm. At last Deakin sat up and spoke:

"So what next?"

"I'll get arrest warrants issued for Deeming and Danby first thing tomorrow morning. Then we'll go into West End Central for the formal interview. I'll get my D.S. to conduct it. I'll be on the carpet, so –"

"Can I doss down here then?"

"Looks like it."

Deakin stood and walked over to the couch, spreading his little body along its length.

"Got my blanket?"

"I binned it."

Deakin nodded and rolled his jacket up under his head for a pillow and laid the huge old Warm across his wretched body. He appeared to drop into sleep almost immediately. Rake turned the fire off and switched off the light before undressing and climbing between the sheets. He wound his clock and set the alarm, before dozing off at some point after midnight. When he awoke the light was beginning to ease itself into the room. Rake raised his head and looked over at the couch. Of course, Deakin was gone.

Alfie spent the night on a bench in Loxford Park and dawn found him shaking with cold and wetted to his marrow. He walked towards Barking Station, buying a bacon sandwich and a mug of tea at the Regent café en-route, and then he stood in a doorway on Station Parade, sheltering, smoking, chewing gum, waiting. Sophie went by at just past eight, heading to her job in Hackney. She was hurrying, trotting really to escape the rain. He called her name, softly so as not to startle her, but she was startled and a lightening array of emotions passed over her face until she gathered herself, her eyes hardening, her mouth pursed. It was an expression he knew well, though he'd never felt so ill equipped to summon a response. They talked, her first and full throttle, him defensive and grave. In the end he was holding her by her arms, holding her really at bay. It was only then that she quietened, as people passed looking at the strange emotive display. At two young people, barely grown, caught in some unfathomable disarray, children acting as adults – what could the problem be, surely not a matter of life and death?

They went by train to the Caledonian Road. They stopped outside a block of flats and Alfie walked stealthily along a narrow passageway and carefully pulled a loose brick from the wall. He reached inside, patting around; he went up on his toes and tried to look into the cavity. Then he ran his hand roughly along the vacant hole.

"Shit!"

"You looking for these, boy?"

Alfie turned. A police constable stood in front of him dangling two keys on a metal ring in his right hand. Alfie watched the keys swinging there before him, mesmerised. Then the policeman shot out his left hand, and shimmering sparks of light exploded inside Alfie's head before he fell into darkness.

Danby was enjoying his breakfast: fried eggs, bacon, black pudding, a Lincolnshire sausage, beans and fried bread. All washed down with builder's tea, two fried breakfasts on two consecutive days, lovely! He was being spoilt, old Basil was looking after him good and proper, like old times, like the good times. This was even better than the café breakfast he'd had yesterday, not swimming in grease, not squirting fat every time he cut into the sausage. Basil walked from the public bar into the snug and whistled through his teeth, miming that Danby was wanted on the phone. Had to be Jimmy or Frank, no one else knew he was dossing down at the pub. He took a big swig of tea, walked back to the hallway and picked up the receiver. He waited. It was Frank.

"You alone?"

"What's up?" Danby was suddenly tense, aware all of a sudden that he was still in jeopardy, a feeling that he'd done well to siphon off or at least split away.

"I'm still at the flat. I was just putting the keys back when I saw this toe rag looking in the brickwork. Anyway, I biffed him. Says his name is Alfie, got a little scrubber with him. I've got them tucked up in the bedroom. Don't know what you want me to do."

"Did you get the passport?"

"No problem, and I got that bit of scratch. What do you want me to do about these two?"

Danby exhaled, hesitated – but only for a moment. Fuck them, I mean really, why was it his problem? It wasn't was it, I mean – was it?

"What are they doing there?"

"How am I supposed to know? Look he's shuffling about at my elbow, you talk to him."

"Mister Danby? It's Alfie."

"Yes, and?"

Danby knew immediately that Alfie had messed it up, shot absolutely everything to hell. Frank could likely have moved in and out in his old uniform with little or no bother, but not Alfie, not likely. He realised that the boy was talking down the line - he hadn't been listening.

"Come again?"

"I don't know what to do, Mister Danby. Her brothers wouldn't let her go; they think they can deal with Deeming. I had to get her away, I mean, what was I supposed to do? Mister Danby? I mean *you* told me to leave, remember?"

Danby breathed into the receiver. He was thinking fast, everything tumbling about, like clothes in a dryer.

"Put Frank on."

"But Mister Danby!"

"Put him on, Alfie."

Frank came back on the line, calm and steady, as ever. His voice helped soothe Danby, at least momentarily.

"You need to get out of there double quick. Just bung them a score out of the wedge and get back here."

"What if they won't leave?"

"Frank, just get out."

Danby heard a voice, hollering: The door! The door! Or something like it. The receiver was dropped, there was scuffling, a thud, a scream – girlish – Sophie maybe, or even Alfie. Everything went quiet, all of a sudden, as if a radio had been turned off. Then the receiver was picked up. Danby could hear breathing down the line. He waited. He noticed that his hand was shaking. He fought to steady his breathing. He was expecting

Deeming, but it wasn't Deeming. It was a low gravelly baritone, reaching down the line like a bitter wind.

"Hello Danby, nice little apartment you've got, nicely appointed, bijou, very smart, neat too eh? Right little housefrau you are."

"Hello Lenny, all right?"

"Very good, no flies on you, yet. I made a joke, did you get it?"

"What do you want?'

"I want you. Oh, I've got your passport here, shit photo; you look like a fucking accountant. Anyway, I've got it here. And these, what are they? George, ask that boy what he is."

Danby heard a cry: Alfie – and an accompanying scream: Sophie. He arched his neck back and clicked the bones, one way and then the other.

"The copper, what's that, Halloween costume? I'm afraid he can't come to the phone; his mouth is full of blood. So then, how do you want to play it?"

"What are the options?"

"You come to the good old Marylebone any time after two tomorrow morning and collect your passport. Or you tell me where you are and I'll post it to you."

"What about them?"

"The boy is fucked. I haven't made my mind up about the girl. Mind you, she'll be fucked whatever, know what I mean?" The last few words came with a hollow laugh, or something like it.

"I'll come to you then, shall I?"

"That's very considerate, very accommodating. Thank you."

The line buzzed. Danby hung up the receiver. The sausage came into his mouth on a river of bile and he swallowed hard. He exhaled. Basil was in the doorway, he shrugged questioningly, and Danby shook his head slowly from side to side.

He walked up to his room and opened the new suitcase. The only thing he extracted was the Webley.

Lenny Matta turned and faced the three hostages, crowded together on the small couch. Frank was in a fugue state, his face already swelling, both eyes bloodshot and oedematous. Alfie Atkins had blood and mucus around his nostrils; he was looking at Matta contemptuously, sitting up straight, rigid, coiled like a heavy spring. Sophie was holding his shoulder, and though tears were welling in her eyes, there was anger there too, it surprised Matta, and it bothered him, though he didn't let it register in any obvious way. George Erskine sat in the armchair holding a heavy Enfield revolver on his lap. He was staring at Sophie, his dark face impassive, save for a lascivious wetness to his lips. Alfie stood suddenly and everyone except for Frank tensed. Sophie reached for the tail of his jacket, but he shook her off and stepped forward.

"So I'm fucked, right? All right, but let her go, she's got nothing to do with this."

Matta raised his heavy black brows and narrowed his deep-set violet eyes. A smile played on his lips and the pink tip of his tongue showed between his teeth. His extraordinary beauty had always been a mixed blessing, it confused people, and they mistook his physical presence for effeminacy until they heard his voice, which had a graveyard resonance and until they saw him in action, when the precision of his violence left them in no doubt as to what he was.

"You know, Alfred – I don't know what it is that Deeming wants from you, do you? Or the skirt, or that," indicating Frank. "I was just hired to get Danby. You're collateral damage to be honest, but here we are. Sorry and all that, you know how it is, wrong time, wrong place, your hard luck, my good fortune – or not, depending how it plays out," he looked at his watch. "Got a day ahead of us and most of the night, before I meet Danby at the club. We can spend it here, I suppose, in the warm, in comfort. Then George and me will trot off and leave you here. That's one possibility. But to be honest I think the other option is looking preferable."

Matta walked over to Frank Hanley and cut him on both sides of his neck, expertly severing the carotid artery and stepping back to avoid the blood. Sophie screamed and scrambled from the couch onto and along the floor, cowering finally at Alfie's feet.

"You'd better shut that cunt up right now, son. Or she's next."

Alfie crouched and held Sophie, trying desperately to quieten her. George Erskine stood and walked over to the decanter and poured himself a whisky.

"Transmission will resume after a short intermission," he said, toasting the room.

The only sound now was a kind of breathy whistle, which escaped Frank in an ever-decreasing beat as he died. That and an occasional sob, loud and harrowing, coming from the girl, wretched in her shock and bewilderment and the traffic, far off on the Caledonian Road, out there – it seemed to Alfie Atkins, in the real world.

# Chapter Eleven

The warrant came through at ten fifteen on Wednesday morning and Rake figured they'd pick Danby up first. From what Norman Balon had said, it was possible that Danby and Deeming had had some kind of falling out, so it made sense to see if he was ready to be even more indiscreet in a formal interview. Sweet drove Rake and a uniformed constable to the Caledonian Road at eleven forty. They walked the janitor up to Danby's flat with the master key, but found that they didn't need it. The door had been jimmied. Rake sent the janitor packing, then he pushed the door open and they entered the flat. The living room appeared to be empty, the blinds shut, and the lights turned off. Rake switched the lights on and took a few steps into the room. The couch was sodden with blood. There was blood on the carpet and it was smeared for ten feet along the floor. Rake walked through to the bedroom, noticing blood and further drag marks, probably made by the heel of a boot. He pushed open the bathroom door. There in the bath was a body, in uniform, the helmet placed over the face of the corpse. He lifted the helmet and turned to his companions.

"Recognise him?"

They both shook their heads, and Rake carefully placed the helmet back over the dead man's face.

"Right, carefully re-tread your steps and wait in the hall." He walked into the living room and placing his handkerchief over the receiver, he phoned West End Central and briefed Harper, calling for an all points bulletin for the arrest of Danby, roadblocks and checks at railway and bus stations and the airport. He then rang through to CID to set up forensics. He walked into the hallway and spoke to the constable, telling him to ensure that the entrance was secured and to remain there until given further instructions. He indicated for Sweet to follow him and headed off to arrest Deeming. As they walked down to the street he stopped on a landing and spoke to the D.S. in an unusually confidential manner.

"You all right?"

"Yes, why?"

119

"That was Frank Hanley, you didn't recognise him?"

"No, I said didn't I?"

"Oh, only he was at Bethnal Green same time as you, wasn't he? Got the elbow for corruption in fifty-seven, fifty-eight. Didn't ring a bell?"

"I didn't know him that well, was it him, really?"

"Really."

"No, no – to be honest I didn't look too closely, I don't like dead bodies."

"All right, well that was definitely Frank Hanley. Give it some thought, eh? Another thing, do you know Harry Bender?"

"Bender? Yes, the Bender's, out of Catford - why?"

"I just heard, he was done in last night in Blackheath, a stabbing apparently. We'll head off then, to Mayfair – get a couple of Woodentops to meet us at Deeming's gaff."

Rake turned and continued on his downward journey, quite buoyed up by the discomfiture of the policeman trotting in his wake.

Danby got into London at three in the afternoon. He left the Consul at Lee and walked in the direction of the train station. He picked up a copy of the Daily Mirror and folded it under his arm, heading to a café to get a coffee and something sweet to eat. Lighting a cigarette he opened the newspaper. Slap bang on the front page was a screaming headline:

### Murder On The Eighth Tee
**Corpse found mutilated on Golf Course**
**The lifeless remains of Harold Bender were discovered early this morning by ground staff at the Blackheath Golf Club.**

He read the story with interest and alarm. Clearly Deeming had gone over the edge. This obviously bode ill for the festivities to come that night. Unconsciously he put his hand into his inside coat pocket and fingered the reassuring weight that rested there. He bit into his cinnamon bun, but it tasted like bitter sand in his dry mouth, so he took a swift gulp of tea and walked to the station. On the train into town he tried to order his thinking. He didn't know what had happened to Frank, or the kids. He knew enough about Lenny Matta to know that he wouldn't hesitate to kill them, but then again, they might be kept as bargaining chips, he'd have them frightened into absolute compliance. He decided to leave the train at the Edgware Road in case they were watching the station at Baker Street. He booked a room at a small hotel and went to the bar for a couple of stiff ones. At five he asked the reception clerk to make sure he got an alarm call at eleven, though he knew he'd be lucky to sleep, and went up the stairs to his room. It was already dark, so he left the curtains open and lay down on the counterpane. The sound of cars and buses, wending their way through the wet street was soothing, and he found himself drifting towards sleep. He checked the gun once more and slid it under his pillow. Poor old H.H., he thought, funny little fellow. Then he was lost in a dream.

Danby slept for less than an hour, then he lay smoking, trying in vain to come up with some strategy that might see him survive until dawn. But it was a conundrum, all he could envisage was Matta's face, the face and a room and the bloom of something red blossoming in those violet eyes. It had been a long time since Danby had felt fear, but it came absolute and vivid, a remnant of his youth, of his emasculated childhood. A time before he'd learned that he could exploit his size and his presence to vanquish threat, to subdue and control other people. He had to get a grip. At eleven the phone rang. He answered and replaced the receiver gently in its cradle. Then he showered and shaved. Wrapped in a thin bath towel he knelt over the toilet and pushed his fingers down his throat, but his stomach was empty and only a thin ribbon of bile came up. He dressed and walked down to the bar, swilling with a single shot of malt to clean his mouth. Then he walked from the hotel and took a taxi to Marylebone.

Deeming hadn't been at the Mayfair flat when Rake had called. He and Sweet returned to Savile Row and busied themselves until they got word that Deeming had been picked up at Simpsons, where he'd been dining with some associates. By the time he'd been processed and his brief had arrived it was gone midnight. Rake took Sweet to the canteen and they discussed strategy over a meal of Cottage Pie and strong tea, letting the man stew in his own juices for a good long while. Then they ambled down to the interview suite.

Deeming and his brief, Whittaker, were waiting, a uniformed constable standing sentinel by the door. Rake indicated for the constable to leave and sat opposite Deeming while Sweet prepared himself to take notes. Rake went through preliminary introductions; Deeming looked at his watch impatiently and sighed.

"Got somewhere to be?" Rake asked.

"I've always got somewhere to be."

Whittaker leaned in and spoke conspiratorially in Deeming's ear, and put his hand over his client's fist. Deeming drew his fist away, but nodded, grunting.

"My client wishes it to be known that he objects most ardently to the way he has been treated, and that I intend, on his behalf, to raise the matter with some urgency with Sir Joseph, who is a personal friend."

"Finished?" Rake interrupted. "Mister Deeming, you were required to attend this interview to help us with our enquiries regarding the murder of Logan Frazer. Frazer was killed on or about the twenty first of December last year. You were, I believe a friend of Frazer's."

"So you're Rake."

Rake widened his eyes and smiled. Then he shuffled through some papers and looked back at Deeming.

"You went on a trip to Tangier with Frazer in November of last year, where you also associated with Charles Goole, Phillip Fry, Maurice Cohen, Patrick Gupta and Roy Huff. You might recollect the event, it was the night that Roy Huff took his own life. Do you?"

"Do I what?"

"Do you remember?"

"No comment."

"Do you know someone by the name of Danby?"

Deeming shrugged and took a sidelong look at Whittaker, who shook his head.

"No comment."

122

"Danby quoted your name in an altercation with Norman Balon, the landlord of the Coach and Horses public house in Greek Street, Soho. He intimated that he was an employee of yours. He suggested that you were likely to pay him, Balon, a visit. It felt to Balon as though this was a threatening, or let me say an intimidating suggestion.  No, all right, do you know where we might find Danby? I see, have you had a tiff? You may have heard that we are keen to see Danby. Have you?"

"Have I what?"

"Heard that Danby is being sought?"

"No comment."

"What about the tiff?"

"Arseholes."

"Did you know that Danby was being sought in connection with a murder? It's been on the news. An ex police officer was found dead in his flat this morning, Danby's flat. You know the one, off the Caledonian Road."

Rake picked a small address book from the table and tossed it across to Deeming.

"Couple of your clubs in there. Not your number of course, I assume he knows that one by heart."

"You not going to ask me about John Deakin?"

Rake struggled to keep his expression from freezing on his face. He had a vision, immediate and tangible in his mind. It was a vision of a table, turning.

At twelve thirty Danby stood in a doorway in Melcombe Place and watched the comings and goings from the Marylebone Yacht Club. He didn't see Matta, so figured he was already in situ, waiting. He stood for an hour, stamping his feet against the cold, holding his face taut to prevent his teeth from chattering. Then there was a sudden exodus from the venue, several cliques, all male, leaving and heading off through the rain towards Dorset Square, where they were more likely to find taxi's. Shortly thereafter the lights went out, or were dimmed certainly, and he knew it was time. He walked across the road and took a few steps along the alleyway that led to the back of the club. Looking round to make sure he wasn't being observed, he carefully propped the Webley behind some bins, as he knew he'd be searched as soon as he entered the building. Then he walked down into darkness towards the rear door and pushed it open.

Deeming reached into his inside jacket pocket and, with a flourish, produced a passport. He fondled it, looking across at Rake, holding his eyes, a smile – or a grin perhaps, playing about the corner of his mouth.

"John Deakin, what, you gone blank?"

"Who's John Deakin?" Sweet asked, looking from Deeming to Rake.

"He's a low life, proper ponce, and he's a homosexual. Isn't that right Chief Inspector? You should know, right? He's been dossing down with you in your apartment, hasn't he? Sleeping in your one room flat, with you, right? Oh, and how's the wife? I understand she's in the loony bin, took an overdose, kicked you out because she thinks you're a pouf, and then tries to kill herself. Well, that's what the word is, that's the word on the jungle drums. Your D.S. looks a bit bewildered Mister Rake. You should have given him the heads up, I mean – I thought you'd have briefed him before you started this whole rigmarole. Bit thoughtless, what? Coming in here half cocked."

At this, Deeming flipped the passport across the table towards Rake.

"Have a flick through, go on, take a deco, do some work for once. I was in Spain from the fourteenth of December right through to Christmas Eve. It's stamped, right? I had a lovely time, wasn't exactly hot, but it was sunny, nice in the day, had to have a woolly though in the evening, it got a bit nippy after five. Marbella, I was staying with John Lambert and his wife, you know John, always on the telly, and the wife, Lady whatshername – posh cow, bit of a lush to be honest. Anyway, they'll vouch for me, basically because, well – that's where I was. Now I do know, because I've done my homework; that Logan Frazer was at Television Centre on the eighteenth of December watching one of his Herbert's singing on a kiddies programme. So, barking up the wrong tree Mister Rake, sorry."

Rake sat as still as a petrified tree, whilst his mind was exploding, the walls crumbling about him. His mouth was vacuumed dry and he could feel the flush of blood travelling from his throat to his cheeks. Sweet reached across him and took up the passport. He flicked through it, and then he tossed it back to Deeming.

"So then Chief Inspector," Whittaker said behind a smile. "If that will be all."

He stood and collected his papers, slipping them into his briefcase and walking towards the door. Deeming sat for a couple of long moments, enjoying himself, enjoying the sense of having vanquished the policeman, relishing the execution, its manner and its consequence. Then he rose, took up the passport and nodded to Sweet.

"We still intend to take this up with the Commissioner first thing in the morning, you've got a few hours to get in there first, son. I'd suggest a letter. He's fucked, but you might have a chance to rescue your career. Up to you, of course."

Deeming joined Whittaker at the door, they exited talking loudly, sharing the joke. Rake and Sweet sat in silence. Then Rake stood and gathered his notes, his hand was trembling noticeably, and when he spoke his voice was a strangled whisper.

"Just put the report in to Harper," he said, "you won't need a letter". Then he walked from the room, leaving Sweet to figure it out for himself.

Danby walked purposefully along the corridor and through the door that led to the small bar in the back room of the Yacht Club. George Erskine was standing behind the counter, just to Danby's right as he entered the room. Erskine had heard the footsteps and had his revolver cocked and ready in his hand. He held it under Danby's chin as he patted him down, he was rough and pushy, but Danby didn't seem to mind. Lenny Matta was sitting at a table eating a steak and drinking red wine. Alfie and Sophie were sitting either side of him. Erskine nodded and Matta pointed at a chair opposite to where he was eating. The chair had been pulled ten feet or so away from the table. Erskine shoved

Danby toward the chair and pushed him, with unnecessary vigour, down onto the seat. Alfie looked at Danby, an expectant, hopeful expression creasing his brow. Sophie looked bedraggled, her long auburn hair dishevelled, falling about her face, making her look even younger than she was. Her blouse was askew, and had been buttoned incorrectly. Danby knew that Erskine had been at work. Matta continued eating, masticating each mouthful as if it were truly delicious, so flavoursome that it preoccupied him beyond the matter at hand.

"Get on with it you little tart, " Danby said.
Erskine jabbed the revolver into Danby's temple, making him wince, but nothing more. Matta cut a slice of steak and put it into his mouth. He pointed at his closed lips and shook his head, as if watching his manners. After he'd swallowed he spoke.

"Waiting for Deeming," he said, before cutting another piece of meat and forking into his maw. He swallowed and laid the cutlery neatly on the table.

"It's been a while, "he said addressing Danby. "You've lost weight, it ages you."

"Where's Deeming?"

"No idea. He was meeting some people up West; I suppose he's stopped off for a little drinkie. I'm sure he's on his way."

"What about Frank?"

"Frank?"

"He was at my flat when you popped by."

"Oh, him, well no – he won't be joining us."

"He's dead Mister Danby," Alfie broke in. "He killed him."
Danby nodded, then he turned his eyes toward Sophie and spoke to her, his voice calm and reassuring.

"You holding up okay?"
Sophie shrugged, only just containing the anger that was clearly welling up along with the tears that she was trying hard to restrain. Alfie reached across the table to where her hand rested, but Matta swatted him off as he might a fly that had landed on his food.

"You dirty bastard," Alfie said through gritted teeth.
Erskine coughed up a laugh, Matta backhanded Alfie across his

mouth and Erskine laughed harder. It was this laughter that sound tracked the chaos that ensued. Sophie picked the steak knife from the table and stuck it into Matta's neck. Matta sprang to his feet as if forcibly ejected from his seat. His eyes were as big as a Tarsier's, the sclera pinking visibly as were his teeth, the rictus flooding with blood. Danby grabbed Erskine by his wrist and jerked down. The revolver went off, the bullet going into the floor, then Danby rose and twisted the arm hard into a half nelson, forcing it up Erskine's back, popping his shoulder from its socket with the violence of its trajectory. The gun clattered to the floor. Danby had him now, his forearm rigid across his windpipe. Sophie stepped swiftly across the room clutching the knife and stuck it into Erskine's stomach, the handle breaking in her hand, the blade protruding an inch from the big man's gut. Danby pushed Erskine away and he fell to the floor as Landau poked his head into the room. Picking up the revolver Danby ushered him in.

"Who the fuck are you?" Danby said.
Landau looked round the room in shock. He took in the body of Erskine, slumped face down on the filthy linoleum, and Matta, spraying blood with each beat of his failing heart, and Sophie, screaming like a banshee, whirling, bloody and lost in her rage.

"I'm the manager," he croaked, finally looking at Danby. "I'm just -" his voice trailed away into the ether.

"Well," Danby said, and he shot him. Then he walked over to Matta and shot him in his heart. The small room reverberated with the whip like crack of the revolver.

"Sort her out," he said to Alfie. "Time to go."
He headed down to the door that led to the hallway and the alley beyond. He collected the Webley, and hearing the door crashing open and their footsteps following, he lit out towards Melcombe Place and the refuge of the city.

It was nearing three thirty when Deeming, accompanied by Vernon and Danieli, walked down the alley and into the small back room. The smell of cordite was the first thing he noticed as he entered the room. He looked about him, his eyes widening and his jaw dropping, he had to refrain from uttering some shape of ridiculous cartoonish oath. After a moment he shrugged his shoulders and walked through the door, following the path that Danby had trodden, only an hour before.

They dropped Danieli at his digs in Paddington and drove to Mayfair. Vernon parked the Magnette but kept the motor running, assuming that Deeming had finished with him for the night. But the big man told him to follow him into the mansion block and they rode the lift together in a frosty silence. As soon as they entered the flat Deeming smelled cigarette smoke and thought of Danby. He flipped the light switch and stalked along the passage and into the lounge. Rake was sitting in an armchair, the onyx ashtray spilling cigarette butts, and a glass of Cognac in his hand.

"How'd you get in?"

"A Warrant Card and my natural authority, the concierge and I met earlier today when I had a uniform with me. Take a seat, and you, what's your name?"

"Vernon."

"Well Vernon, pour us all a nice brandy, eh? Then you can go off home to your mum."

Vernon looked to Deeming, but Deeming was focused absolutely on the policeman. Vernon walked to the trolley and collected the decanter, he poured a drink for Deeming and handed him the glass.

"Shall I?"

Deeming nodded and Vernon carried the decanter to Rake and topped up his drink. When he replaced the decanter he quietly exited the lounge. They heard the front door close.

"Nice looking lad," said Rake.

"What do you want?" Deeming said, he sat heavily in an armchair.

"Well, I'm still a copper Mister Deeming, still a copper, eh? I've got around five hours I reckon, until I'm suspended, so I thought – why not? Why not? Why not have a reckoning with you, you slimy fat cunt?"

"Hard man, are you? Going to rough me up a bit?" A nasty grin cracked his pendulous face, and then it was switched off like a light bulb. "Go on then, what?"

Rake sipped his drink and laid the glass on the floor at his feet. He took out a pack of Craven A and proffered it to Deeming, but Deeming just carried on looking at him, inscrutable and flaccid in the big armchair. Rake lit a cigarette and reached into his coat pocket pulling out the brass knuckles.

"Recognise these?" Rake waited, nothing came back. "They belong to your oppo, Danby. I took them off him. We're still looking for him, the murder in his flat, we spoke about it."

"I didn't."

"No, that's right, I stand corrected – I spoke about it. Any news?" Still nothing. "All right, what about Logan Frazer?"

"I was in Spain."

"You were, yes, you were in Spain. It was cool in the evening and you needed your cardie, didn't you? But you instructed Danby to murder him?"

"Why would I?"

"Because he owed you money, because he set you up to have sex with an underage boy and you were being blackmailed by him. You must remember, Roy Huff – Little Mickey Magnet, sixteen years old. You would remember I'm sure, after all, the kid topped himself."

"I didn't have anything to do with Logan Frazer's death."

"Where's Danby?"

"I wish I knew."

"We'll find him and we'll break him."

"We? There is no we anymore Rake, you're finished, you're a landed fish, gasping, stranded, it's fun to watch but I'm tired, so finish your drink and fuck off."

"You are responsible for the death of Roy Huff."

"I don't know what you're talking about. Is this John Deakin, he been bending you ear? Your dirty little secret, eh? Is it? He's a filthy liar and you know it, he's ruined you, hear that clock ticking? It's counting down your life. It'll get in the papers, about you being a pouf. They won't spell it out, but it'll be there, between the lines, in the News of the World. Too many people know. You'll be a suicide, just like your wife. How is she doing? I hear she's out of hospital, poor cow."

"I just want to know about Logan Frazer."

"It don't matter, he's dead and that's that."

"It matters to me."

"You ever think that you might be mental?"

Rake stood and slipped the brass knuckles into his pocket.

"When this is all done, I'll be back for you."

"When what's done? It's like what my old girl used to say, she said empty vessels make the most noise."

"I'll be a civilian soon Deeming, then we can have a proper little chinwag"

"I'll look forward to it. Make an appointment though, I'm very busy."

Rake walked out of the apartment and into another piercing London dawn. He pointed his body towards Soho and the Charing Cross Road and started walking. He was aware that blackbirds were starting to sing in the park, spring was coming; soon there would be snowdrops.

# Chapter Twelve

The Narrow Boat was big, seventy-two feet, and it was dilapidated, a floating hovel. It listed heavily on the port side, making it feel to Deakin that he was drunk, though unusually, he hadn't imbibed that morning. He and Farson had run out of alcohol and it had been too cold and too wet to venture into Limehouse to buy a bottle the previous evening. They'd sat arguing about who should go, until they were timed out. He looked over towards the galley, where Farson was frying black pudding and slipping the greasy roundels between slices of thick white bread. He walked haphazardly over to Deakin's bunk and deposited the sandwich onto the blanket. He looked down at the little man and ran a pudgy hand through his luxurious blonde fringe.

"I've got to go to the studio this morning, John."
"Oh look at me, I've got to go to the studio."
Deakin picked up the sandwich, looked at it, smelled it and dropped it on the floor. He laid his head back on the pillow and closed his eyes.

"Isn't David's flat available? I'm going to lock up when I go."
"So? Just lock me in. I haven't anywhere to go Dan. I can't go to Bayswater, David is a bit off with me, I told you."

Farson sighed, exasperated. Deakin had turned up in the early hours a couple of days before, and whilst Farson liked and admired Deakin as a photographer and enjoyed his company, it was only in small doses and he had reached the end of his tether. He bent down and picked up the sandwich, walking through the wall deck doors and flipping it into the basin's murky water. He took in the misty glory of that early morning, enjoying the ramshackle panorama, ancient and galvanizing, beautiful in his minds eye – then he turned his face towards Deakin, and shuddered. A foghorn blasted some way off, out there in the hazy grey estuary; he took it as an omen, a signal of farewell. He stiffened his resolve and turned to face the mite. He took a few pounds from his trouser pocket and, in passing; he laid the notes onto Deakin's bunk. It's what Deakin had been angling for, and he swung his pale emaciated legs from the bedding and stood. He counted the money and poked it into the pocket of his Warm. Reaching for his trousers he nodded over at the galley.

"I'll have one of those sandwiches, please. I seem to have recovered an appetite."

The Narrow Boat trimmed noticeably as a large vessel steamed by and Deakin took two steps forward and a long step back to steady himself, one leg flapping into his trousers. Unperturbed, Farson began to make up a sandwich, watching from the corner of his eye as Deakin hopped about trying to get into his breeches. Neither man had an inkling that Farson would, two decades later, chronicle the little fellow's life in print, rekindling an interest in his work, his psyche and his milieu. He slipped two slices of pudding between thickly buttered bread and took it over to Deakin. Deakin saluted him with the sandwich and headed out of the cabin, humming tunelessly, some faded ditty from his Liverpool childhood.

Rake stopped off for breakfast at the New Piccadilly Café in Denman Street and treated himself to a fried egg laid over bubble and squeak with two fat sausages on the side. Then he walked back to the Charing Cross Road and climbed up the stairs to his room. The door was closed, obviously held in place by some obstacle, as the lock still hadn't been fixed. He thought of Deakin and pushed the door open quite casually. Danby was sitting at the table with a mug of coffee in his hand. Rake faltered, confused – a feeling that mounted as he looked over at his bed. A young man was sitting there, his hand resting on the sleeping form of a girl who was wrapped in a blanket. One small hand was resting on the boys lap. The hand was caked with dried blood. He looked back at Danby, who sipped at his coffee, wholly nonchalant and in control.

"Your wife has been on the blower, says for you to give her a bell, sharpish."

"I've been looking for you."

"Well, you've found me, cock."

Rake pulled up a chair and sat opposite Danby. He looked over at the young couple.

"Who?"

"That's Alfie Atkins and his better half, Sophie something. They need protection. Deeming's looking for them; he's after a bit of mischief. They'll need a brief and some breakfast. You'll take care of them, be a promotion in it I shouldn't wonder."

Danby stood and collected his cigarettes. Rake stood to face him; he pushed his hand into his coat pocket and came up with the knuckle-dusters, laying them carefully on the table.

"I'm arresting you on suspicion of the murder of Frank Hanley."

Danby pulled the Webley from his coat and pointed it loosely in the direction of Rake's midriff.

"Look, that won't wash, it was a bloke called Lenny Matta. Matta's dead, self-defence, he's at the Marylebone Yacht Club. I shot him. These two witnessed Matta killing Frank on Deeming's orders; him and me are on the outs. He's lost it, gone berserk."

"I know."

"Right, well you should have pulled the fucker in then, no? Look, these two need to be kept safe. I'm guessing it's the least you can do."

"Did you kill Logan Frazer?"

Danby looked genuinely surprised. He shook his head and walked towards the splintered door.

"You want to get some food in here, oh, and you'd better ring the wife, she sounded a bit hysterical. Frank Hanley was a very good friend of mine by the way, and I didn't kill Frazer. You're not very good at your job, Mister Rake, and I'll have the knucks, you shouldn't be brandishing them, very unbecoming."

Rake shrugged and Danby collected them, smiling. He walked through the door. Rake and Alfie seemed to concentrate in unison on the sound of his footsteps receding, as if the echo held within it some mystery or a peculiar metaphysical significance. At the sound of the street door closing their eyes met.

"What are you going to do?" Alfie enquired.

"I'm going to phone the station and then I'm going to ring my wife, son. Then I'll take you to West End Central. Don't say another word until your brief turns up. Have you got someone?"

Alfie shook his head. Rake nodded, then he went to the phone and dialled through to West End Central and updated Sweet, instructing him to get a bulletin about Danby on the wire urgently, ignoring the surprise in the man's voice. Then he dialled through to the house in Putney that he'd once called home.

Deakin got off the bus at Leicester Square and looked at the traffic on the Charing Cross Road waiting for a gap. When he saw the lights change further down the thoroughfare he took a step but he halted, frozen, as he spied Danby coming from the alley that led to Rake's building. Danby started to cross the road but turned his head at that moment and their eyes met as the lights changed to green. Deakin spun and ran towards Lisle Street. He could hear the sound of Danby's blakeys cracking on the road behind him, and the urgent squeal of brakes accompanying a blasting horn, roaring up the street, as if he were being pursued by a hellhound. He turned left, his heart pumping, his tarred lungs struggling to take in oxygen, he thought he might faint. He stopped at last and turning he raised his fists, just as Danby reached him. Deakin could hardly lever enough wind to call out, but he did, managing each wheezed word on an outward breath.

"Come on then you leery cunt."
Danby slowed, raising his hands, palm outward, defensive and placatory – gently pushing at air. He halted twenty feet from Deakin. He shook his head.

"No, it's all right, mate. I'm not after any bother, I just want to talk."

Deakin kept his stance, his eyes darting, looking for a way out. Danby took another step forward; he was aware that pedestrians were passing the street only yards away and he imagined he could hear a siren in the distance, approaching.

"What about we go somewhere, somewhere lively? I'll get you breakfast."

"I've had my breakfast."

"Well I haven't. Look, we can settle this nice and easy. I don't work with Deeming anymore, I'm in the same position as you."

"Don't make me laugh."

"Seriously, I can make it all go away. Have you still got the negatives?"

Deakin thought about that, for a full twenty seconds. He relaxed the stance a tad and leaned against a wall.

"What were you doing at Rake's flat?"

"I had to drop a couple of kids off to him," he took another step. "Deeming's driver and his Judy, it's a long story and I haven't got time. I need the negatives and I need to know what it was all about. I've seen the photograph's, right? They nailed the coffin shut on Deeming and me. You can phone Rake, ask him. Have you seen the papers?"

"No, what about it?"

"Old H.H. Bender got himself skewered, he's dead. Sure to be Deeming, you want to think about it. You'll be next, you need to find a hidey-hole, let me help, I've got contacts."

"Did you tell Rake?"

"I'm not a grass, let him work it out, but you're in the karzy, John."

Deakin rubbed his eyes with his nicotine fingers; his breathing was slowing, though he felt nauseous and bone weary to his boots.

"What's it worth?"

"I've got a score, you can have it."

"Up front."

"Can I trust you?"

"Of course not, you berk."

"Thought not," Danby said, and he chinned the little man with a short sharp jab. Deakin's head hit the wall and he was left semi-conscious as Danby propped him up, his free hand rifling through the pockets of the Warm. He came up with cigarettes, matches, a filthy comb, a filthier handkerchief and a key. He dropped them onto the pavement. He went to Deakin's trousers pulling out some banknotes, which he pocketed, then a soiled, creased envelope. He let go of Deakin who remained standing, coming into consciousness, and opened the envelope. The negatives were in a long thin glassine sleeve. Danby pocketed the booty, spun on his heels and ran up Newport Place into Frith Street. He flagged down a taxi at the corner of Old Compton Street. He imagined he could hear sirens, closer now, but it was only the blood pounding in his ears. He gave the destination to the driver and fell back into the seat. Danby knew that if he could stay free until nightfall, he might still have a chance.

Rake took the two young people to the station in a taxi; the girl still wrapped in the ratty blanket, pale and trembling with a cold that rose from her marrow, Alfie Atkins sheltering her protectively all the while. Rake called a WPC over and instructed her to take them to an interview room and to stay with them. Then he found Sweet and gave him the full run down, leaving out his visit to Deeming's apartment. He instructed the D.S. to get them a solicitor before reading them their rights. Sweet made notes, and then he looked up at Rake and spoke, his voice low and firm.

"I've put the report in. It's on Harper's desk."
"What did he say?"
"He's in a meeting, due back at midday."
"All right, yes, fine. Get me the address for Phillip Fry."
"Why?"
"Just give me the address, Peter," Rake hissed, slapping his palm on the desk. People nearby looked over, Rake faced them and they went back to their work, used to their guvnor's occasional outbursts.
"It was Danby, surely."
"I'm not sure. Fry was next on the list and I intend to finish the job, one way or another."
"For God's sake, you don't know when to stop do you?"
"No, do you? If you do you're in the wrong bloody job."
Sweet went through the paperwork in his in-tray and pulled out a sheet. He copied the address down on his pad and tore the page out, handing it to Rake.
"Do you want me to come?"

"Don't be stupid. Anyway, you can lead the interview with Atkins, get Thompson to sit in with you, all right? Last thing, someone here has obviously leaked to Deeming, any thoughts?" Sweet shook his head. Rake held up the page with the address, he memorised the location and then he screwed it into a ball and threw it into the wastepaper basket.

"I didn't get it from you, Peter."

Rake turned on his heels and left the station, stepping onto Savile Row just as the rain started to fall.

Deeming listened to the rain gusting sporadically against his bedroom window. He'd had too much Cognac. He'd started drinking when Rake left the apartment and had continued through the dawn. When Vernon had returned at ten thirty, Deeming had told the boy to join him for breakfast and they'd finished the Courvoisier over scrambled eggs with smoked salmon. Then he'd taking Vernon to bed and put him through his paces. Vernon was sleeping now, lying on his stomach, his buttocks exposed. Deeming watched him breathing for a few minutes then turned back to the window, looking out at the bleak lead grey sky, a Hangman's Sky, his mother would have called it. Grunting he pulled back the sheet and got up. He looked down at his stomach; he was going to fat, getting soft. His shins ached and his ankles were stiff, he walked as if on stilts over to the window and looked down at the car park, at the Magnette. He missed the Daimler and wondered for a moment where it might be. Then he went into the bathroom and looked at his reflection in the mirror. His dishevelled hair barely covered his pate in places and he felt immediately deflated. He had dreamed that his hair had grown back, it was becoming a recurring theme and he often had a moment, on waking, when he thought it was true. He ran a comb through the sparse matted tangle and then ran water and splashed his face. When he walked back to the bedroom his ankles had loosened somewhat and that made him feel a little better. He heard Carmen rattling around in the kitchen and shouted out for coffee. Then he shook Vernon awake and told him to get dressed and go down to the car and wait.

Having dressed, Deeming went to the phone and called Danieli. He instructed him to pick up Billy Manuel, Terry Barker and Charlie Hurren and to bring them to the apartment at four that afternoon. Then he phoned his barber and told him to get to the apartment at three. When the girl came in to see if he wanted lunch he told her to go home. Finally he made himself a fried egg sandwich and watched a bit of the racing on his television.

Rake got to Phillip Fry's home in Hendon at just past eleven in the morning. He looked for the bell to flat number four and buzzed it. There was no answer, so he buzzed again, keeping his finger on the button. When there was still no answer he set his knuckles to the glass pane and waited. A woman, nice looking he thought, opened the door and asked what he wanted.

"I'm looking for Phillip Fry," he said.

"He went out I think, can I help you?"

Rake showed her his warrant card and asked if she had any ideas as to his whereabouts or expected arrival back home. She shook her head.

"He's hardly ever here really, he's an entertainer you know, quite famous, Johnny Rocket, he's been on the telly, though not so much lately."

"That's right, all done up in leather's."

"He's lovely, nothing like he seems, really nice, not like his image."

"So I've been told."

"Have you? Well it's true; he's a proper gentleman. Helps old Missus McQuaid, she's in number one, not been very well, anyway, he does her shopping when he's here. She always has the same thing, same every day, a sliced loaf, corned beef and a small bottle of White Horse, every single day. My husband does the shop when Mister Fry isn't around."

"Is she at home, the old lady?"

"She's always at home, but she's very confused, you won't get anything out of her, no – you'd probably frighten her actually. She's a bit, a bit simple really."

Rake nodded and took out his card. He crossed out the station number and wrote his personal number on the card.

"Please ask Mister Fry to phone me when he comes back. It's rather important."

"What's he done?" She said, looking alarmed.

"Nothing, no nothing at all. He might be able to help with an investigation, that's all. He's not in any trouble, please reassure him of that when you see him."

"Is this about his manager? He was murdered, wasn't he?" Rake smiled and began to walk back along the path. He turned at the gate and offered a small reassuring wave. He walked down to the Broadway and had a cup of coffee. He mulled over his options. He could of course wait outside the flat to see if Fry turned up, but he might be on the road, he could be anywhere really. He could go back to his room and wait to see if the phone rang, but if it did it might be Harper, calling him in for interview. He lit a Craven A and sat back, pondering. How had it come to this? He was a good copper; well he was, wasn't he? Most policemen had marriage difficulties, didn't they? His big mistake was letting Deakin stay, but then, what was he supposed to do – leave him to perish? But he knew, he knew that there was that thread, that fact, the truth that underpinned the rumours. The party at Hainault when Ruth had got drunk and accused him, shouting at him in the car park, someone had heard, someone had spread the rumour.

He shook off the self-pity, gathered his cigarette packet and his matches and left the café. He walked to Hendon Central, caught a Northern Line train to Leicester Square and headed towards his flat. Deakin was waiting in the alleyway. For the first time since New Years Day he was pleased to see him. He noticed the contusion on his chin.

"Been in the wars?"

"I bumped into friend Danby. He's got the negatives, bloody swine took my money too."

"Do you want a job?"

"What sort of job?"

Rake unlocked his front door and ushered Deakin inside. Now I can be in two places at once, he thought to himself as he followed the ragamuffin up the stairs.

Danby alighted at Marble Arch and strode into Hyde Park. He sat on a bench and looked at his watch, it was only two thirty; it wouldn't be dark for at least another two hours. He considered his options. Yes, all right, he thought and with that thought he propelled himself out of the gates and onto the Bayswater Road. He turned left towards Lancaster Gate and then he crossed the road and entered the guts of Bayswater. He found the Craven Hotel just where he remembered it; it still looked anonymous, seedy and abandoned. The man sitting at the reception desk looked familiar to Danby, which wasn't at all helpful, especially as he noticed a folded copy of the Daily Mail on the counter. However, the man didn't appear to react when he looked at Danby, so he fronted it out.

"Have you got a quiet room, top floor back?"
"Just for tonight?"
"Probably, I don't know yet."
"Business?"
"No, I'm just visiting, holiday, seeing the sights."
"Not local then?"
"No, I'm down from Leeds."
"You got any luggage?"
"At the station, I'll pick them up when I go out."

The man turned the register and found a pen. Danby signed in as R. Black and waited to collect his key. The man went to a long mahogany set of pigeonholes and fished out a large key attached to a wooden fob, but he held on to it, clearly in need of further discourse.

"Where are you off to tonight then," he looked at the register, "Mister Black?"

"Up West, I should think. Would you recommend anywhere for supper?"

"I hear the New Benelux is good, nice supper club, with dancing, if you're after a bit of skirt. I've not been myself, of course. Too busy here, and I've got the wife at home. You married; I notice you haven't got a ring? Free and single, eh? Quite right, don't blame you, mind – I wouldn't be without mine, you know, not for a minute. Thirty five years, got two growned boys, wouldn't be without it, family I mean."

"Good for you." Danby held out his hand and the man handed over the key.

"Breakfast is from seven thirty to nine thirty, the restaurant is just down them stairs to the left."

"Thanks."

"You want a newspaper?"

"I'll take the Daily Mail."

The man made a note. He looked back at Danby and smiled. Danby smiled back and nodded.

"Any chance I could take a lend of that?" He pointed at the folded newspaper. The man handed it over.

"I'll take it back when you go out, if you don't mind. It's a quiet night and I haven't read it yet."

"Of course," Danby said.

"Up the stairs, third floor, it's a nice room, very quiet." Danby saluted and walked up the stairs to his room. It was as depressing as he remembered, the overhead light was underpowered and it made the room yawn sinisterly, picking out the utility furniture: the colossal wardrobe, dominating the room like a sentinel, the tatty desk, scarred with cigarette burns and the bed, it's buttoned nylon headboard replete with dark greasy stains from the hundreds of brillcreemed heads that had rested upon it. He walked over to the bedside table and switched on the reading lamp, then he turned off the centre light and sat on the bed looked out at the sky. Evening was drawing in and the clouds slowly took on a nacreous glow as the sun began to set over the park. Danby unfolded the newspaper and spread it on the desk, running his eyes down each column. He found it on page two:

### Murder In Islington
**Man's body discovered by police on the Caledonian Road**

**Tenant of flat sought urgently for questioning.**

Danby's name was mentioned twice, but there wasn't a photograph, not yet anyway. The description was accurate and he imagined that a photo-fit or an artist's impression would soon be on the wire. The only photographs taken that he could recall were his passport photo, which Matta had lodged somewhere, and the mug shot taken when he went to Aldershot, which was sixteen years old, when his hair was black and he had no moustache. He was described as armed and dangerous. Fair enough, he thought.

He walked back to the bed and lay down. He checked his watch, in was approaching four, he had time. He stretched out and closed his eyes. His thoughts turned to Frank Hanley. They'd met at school on Canvey, when Danby had joined the class. He'd been thirteen, maybe – or twelve, something like that. His mum had moved to the Island from Basildon, which had been his fault really, him having been expelled from school there. Frank had taken the rise out of him because of his scruffy clothes, calling him a Pikey and so forth, leading a chorus of POV POV POV at morning break. So that first lunchtime Danby had followed him around the playground lobbing stones at his head, bouncing them off his skull one at a time at regular intervals. Frank's friends, after initially supporting him, slowly turned away, one by one, they saw something in Danby that silenced them. Frank saw it too, and soon he was cowed, not even objecting, just taking it, tears welling pitifully in his large blue eyes. Danby had begun to feel sorry for him; he still had that shred, in those days. But he persisted right up until the bell rang for class. At lunch the following day, Frank had asked if he could sit next to Danby. Danby hadn't spoken, but offered instead a nod of assent, like a kind of King's consent. That's how it went for Danby, all through his school days. It disturbed his teachers, but his credibility among peers was well grounded and it sustained him through all the nonsense. Now Frank was dead, because of a favour asked and a favour granted, no questions, no price tag. When Danby woke it was just past eight. Time.

It was as dark as pitch when Danby stepped out of the hotel; he looked up and down the quiet street and began walking back towards the park. He hailed a taxi at Lancaster Gate tube and directed the driver to go to Stratford. The cabbie tried to strike up a conversation, but Danby just sat back in the shadows and remained silent. Eventually the cabbie grunted and held his peace. Danby alighted by the station and walked to the Daimler. He got in and started the engine, it purred wonderfully to life at the first turn of the key. He put it in gear and drove through Mile End, past the destitute ones, picking up vegetables and fruit, left on the street after the long market had closed. He made good time getting to the City, the buildings lit starkly against the inky blackness of the street and the starry marvel of the sky. It would take him less than thirty minutes now, given the hour, to get to Mayfair, to get to Deeming. Within the hour, he thought to himself, one or perhaps both of them might be dead, but his idea was subtler than a killing. He was going to skin Deeming, a layer at a time. Pare him; flay him, like he might a deer. He smiled at his reflection in the rear view mirror. He felt a trifle sorry about the car, he'd become fond of it over time, more fond in fact than he was of any living soul, apart of course from Frank Hanley, Jimmy Watling and good old Basil Cumper. And Frank wasn't living, was he. No, Frank Hanley was dead.

Rake sat at his ratty little table drinking Camp Coffee laced with Vlahov Cherry Brandy, which was all he had available in the flat that evening. His cheese and pickle sandwich sat untouched on the plate and the ashtray overflowed with cigarette butts. He rifled through the debris, found a smokeable butt and lit it, coughing catarrh from his lungs and swallowing the phlegm like he might an oyster. Then the phone rang. Harper hadn't rung all day and this might be him. He looked at his watch, it was nine forty, unlikely to be the guvnor, he hoped. He picked up the receiver and waited, the coins hit the box, it was Deakin.
"Hello?"
"Hello John, is he back?"
"Just went in, looked a bit wobbly, think he's had a few."
"Perfect, lovely. I'm on my way."
"I'll be off then."
"No, you stay there."
"It's brass monkey's, you arse."
"I'm on my way, don't move."
"I'm going in the Mitre, meet me there, you can buy me a drink."
Rake hung up, turned off the electric heater and ran down to hail a taxi on the Charing Cross Road. As soon as he sat down he

realised that he needed the toilet. Well, he thought grimly, I'm going to create a stink anyway, so.

Alfie Atkins sat forlorn and abandoned in an interview room at West End Central. Sophie had kicked up a storm and Declan had come to collect her. She had finished with Alfie, for good and all she had said, and she had meant it. The ferocity in her blue green eyes had robbed the boy of words. In the interview they'd kept to Danby's script, not mentioning their presence at the Marylebone Yacht Club, just concentrating on Alfie's falling out with Deeming and the carnage at Danby's flat. They stated that they had fled when Lenny Matta murdered Frank Hanley, that they'd bumped into Danby on the Caledonian Road and that he had taken them to Chief Inspector Rake for sanctuary. Of course it all sounded like nonsense to Sweet, but he had nothing really to charge them with and their brief made it clear that they were victims, not perpetrators, which was in fact, the truth.

"Charge them or release them," he had said. So Declan had arrived, and in the interval between statements he had taken a moment with Alfie.

"I'll be taking the girl back to Dublin, right boy? And you'll keep your fuckin' nose out of it from now on, hear me boy?"

On the word "boy", he'd poked Alfie in the chest, both times, hard. It had been difficult for Alfie to evade Sweet's questions about why Deeming was so enmeshed with him, so attached that his departure had caused such chaos, the implication was clear, even though Sweet didn't specifically name it due to the solicitors intervention. But Alfie's face, his blushes, his eyes, had betrayed him, and Sophie, he knew, had worked it out - all the pain, the literal pain, and the humiliation, all for nothing, just wreckage now. Sweet had said clearly that they couldn't leave town, that they were witnesses to a killing, but Alfie knew that she was gone; the brother's didn't give a fig, not where Sophie was concerned. She was out of his reach, out of his life, forever - all for nothing, all gone west. Down the plughole, so now it was just him, in that bare room, in that cold stark room, with no one and with nothing.

Detective Sergeant Sweet entered with a cup of tea and sat down opposite Alfie Atkins. He offered a cigarette, but Alfie shook his head.

"Mister Rake said we should offer you a room, you know, keep you out of mischief. It's not much to be honest. In fact it's a cell, but you'll be on your own at least. Want something to eat? Sandwich, sausage roll, it's not the Ritz but it's what we have."

"No you're all right, thanks."

"Got somewhere to go?"

"I'll make out."

"Well, Chief Inspector Rake did say."

"No, thanks. Can I go?"

"What's the address?"

Alfie gave the Belmont Road address and took to his feet. He had pins and needles from sitting so long; he shuffled to get the blood flowing, his eyes flicking to the door, unsure as to the next step. When Sweet collected up his notebook and pen Alfie said "thank you", and walked out of the room. He stepped onto Savile Row, shocked by the bitter rawness of the night. He had no idea as to the time, but the street seemed deserted, so he knew it was late. He probably had enough money to get a night bus east, and then he would walk. He would walk to Ilford; after all, he had nowhere else to go.

## Chapter Thirteen

Danby drove the Daimler into the car park. He braked and pulled up some way away from the other vehicles, in the chevron painted No Parking section, just by the back entrance to the mansion block. He sat, letting the motor idle. He looked up at Deeming's window. There was a figure standing looking out, a silhouette, tall and slim, not Deeming he knew, just one of the chaps. He switched off the engine and took the Webley from his coat pocket and broke it open. The cylinder was full, six shots, he knew it of course, but it was a superstition carried over from the war. He clicked the gun shut and spun the cylinder. It was in good shape. Then he took out the Enfield .38 that he's robbed from Erskine at the Yacht Club. He broke it and checked the cylinder. There were four unspent cartridges and the gun was filthy. It was only any good for short-range combat, but he figured it would all be pretty up close and personal, if the balloon went up. He clicked the weapon shut and climbed out of the Daimler. He dropped the Webley into his pocket and shoved the Enfield into his belt and walked around the car to open the boot.

Billy Manuel watched the Daimler pull into the car park. He watched it idling there under the lights. He watched Danby climb out of the vehicle. He watched Danby open the boot and he watched him extract what looked like a petrol can. He turned to Deeming then, his timing was perfect.

"Here we go," he said. Manuel wanted action; he wanted to know absolutely that there would be no turning back, Danby had to go over the line, if Deeming had a line. Danby had broken Manuel's nose and cracked his cheekbone back there in Belmont Road, and it hadn't set right, leaving him looking like a punchy boxer and speaking like a cleft palate monkey. He was ready for Danby, hopped up on amphetamines and feeling sparky. Barker walked from the bedroom and joined Manuel at the window.

"What's he up to?"

Deeming stood beside them and looked down at the car and the man busying himself with the petrol can. Then they watched as Charlie Hurren climbed out of the red Humber, lofting a gun and aiming it at Danby. He was perhaps twenty yards from his target when he fired. The bullet careened off the roof of the Daimler shooting sparks from the metal. A nanosecond later the report reached the triad.

"Bit lively," said Manuel.

It was precisely at that moment that the flames held and caught, the car burst orange. Hurren covered his face and stumbled back a few steps as Danby calmly walked around the conflagration towards the retreating figure. Danby stood, his face lit infernally, the breath from his nose pluming in the cutting air. He didn't take up either gun; he just looked at Hurren, fire dancing in his eyes. He tilted his chin and spoke, his words falling heavily in the vapour.

"Are you going to die tonight, Charlie boy?"

Hurren stepped back two, three strides, as if skating on thin ice, then he turned on his heels and ran, ducking and weaving into darkness, dodging imaginary bullets. Danby walked back towards the apartment building and looked up. Windows were opening, people were calling out into the night. Soon there would be sirens. Deeming couldn't start shooting from the window, not with the police coming and anonymity denied. There he was, a lone silhouette, his meaty squat frame staring down. Manuel and Barker were on their way down, Danby figured. He walked out of the car park and into Mount Street Gardens. He knew that this was the assembly point, and soon enough he heard the tintinnabulation of the fire alarm underpinned by the anxious ring of police sirens approaching. People began to stream from the mansion block like a mob of meerkats, heads bobbing, some in their dressing gowns others dressed casually, pulling coats around their shoulders against the bitter night. The concierge was corralling them, counting heads, calling names, making notes on a clipboard, enjoying his brief moment of authority. Danby fell back into the shadows cast by a thicket of plane trees. Police cars, two ambulances and a fire engine arrived, jostling for position, blocking the entrance way to the car park, then reversing to allow ingress to the big engine. Then the Daimler's petrol tank caught and there was a loud explosion, the sky turning ochre for a moment before oily black smoke plumed above the building. Heads ducked in unison as if they'd all been clouted by God's own hand, the babble ceased abruptly as all necks swivelled to look at the edifice, and then it started up again, louder, honking, as nasal as a gaggle of geese. He saw Deeming. He came marching across the road, gesticulating at his two lieutenants. Manuel and Barker peeled off, going in search of Danby. The concierge interrupted their progress, officiously attempting to keep them with the group, looking down at his list, and then asking their names. Danieli said something that startled the man, and then he and Barker strode swiftly from the scene, heading in opposite directions. Danby walked from the shadow of the trees, over the grass to the railings and edged his way through the crowd to stand at Deeming's shoulder. After a short moment Deeming sensed a presence. He looked up at Danby, and then looked away. He took a step but Danby kept apace and they found themselves at the fringe of the crowd. Deeming's eyes remained planted, staring across the road, looking at the building.

" You mad cunt," he said. He waited, but got no response. "This is fucking uncivilised, moronic, not like you, you gone mental? You're fucking mental. What's all this old bollocks, eh?" He looked up at Danby. "Cat got your tongue? Nothing to say?"

"I'm going to take everything from you. I'm going to strip you naked in front of the world."

Deeming looked away again and barked a laugh, shaking his head.

"No cunt, not going to happen. What, I lost a motor? I got fucking insurance, you berk; I got motors coming out of my arse. This is, it's a fucking joke, and you're a fucking joke, Danby. Danby?" He looked up once more. Danby wasn't there. He looked around, spun around, shuffled through the people into the depths of the Garden. He felt the tension in his neck. He realised that he was biting down hard on his tongue. He looked to see if Manuel or Barker were nearby, but no, he was quite alone, save for the many neighbours that he had never before acknowledged.

The rain started up again, which was a good omen, keeping people off the streets. It took Danby only thirty minutes to walk to Piccadilly. He found the Eros Cinema on the corner of Shaftsbury Avenue and hustled his way through the rent boys and toms that hung around its extremity, climbing up the stairs to the top floor of the building. There was a door, with frosted glass and the legend: Office, Knock Before Entering, painted in crumbling black letters upon the corrugated facet, he didn't knock, he just walked right in. Jimmy Vella was sitting behind a desk in the poky little room. He looked up scowling as Danby shut the door, then his head lifted, a smile creasing his thin pale face.

"At last, the ghost of Cock Lane, a visitation. Sir, I am most honoured and delighted."

"Hello Jimmy, how's it going?"

Jimmy Vella stood and steered Danby into a chair. He walked back around the desk and opened a drawer, pulling a bottle of Black and White from its depths and laying it amongst the detritus. He poured two large measures and handed one to Danby.

"Things are tickety-boo old habib, top hole, very tkissir, sparkling, you? I been reading about your troubles. Not so good. So, must say Jimmy is surprised to see you, must say so, maybe you need a helping hand, that's what Jimmy is thinking."

"Spot on." Danby reached into his pocket and took out the negatives. He tossed them onto the desk. "Can you get two sets of these printed up?"

"What are they, family snaps, Bognor?"

"Not exactly."

Vella nodded. He sat back and lit the stub of a cigar, waiting. Danby lit a cigarette and took a sip of his whisky.

"They're pictures of Noel Deeming raping a young boy, Roy Huff"

"The pop singer?" Vella exhaled noisily and shook his head in disgust.

Danby nodded and took another sip. He carefully placed the glass on the desk and stood up.

"It's a yes or no, Jimmy. I need two copies and the negatives back and I need it done by morning. There's no money in it, I don't have much cash and I haven't got much time either, so no fucking about, all right? It's a favour, simple as."

Vella's face clouded, he picked up the sleeve, pulled out a strip of film and held it against the desk lamp. He picked a magnifying glass from the desk and spent some time studying the images. Then he slid the strip back into the sleeve and placed it on the desk.

"Bit of a shit, Noel, eh? So, what you going to do with the pictures, ghost, blackmail him? He'll kill you first, right? And what about Jimmy? He finds out…"

Vella drew his long nailed thumb across his throat. He looked up at Danby and shrugged.

" He won't find out, stand on me, Jimmy. And it's not blackmail; I'm not after his money. So, what about it?"

"You expect a lot and you offer little."

"No, I offer nothing."

Vella fiddled with the strip, as if making up his mind, shuffling it to and fro across six inches of desktop.

"Why did you come to me with this?"

"Because you have a darkroom, because you don't sleep at night, because I'm desperate."

"Oh thank you, very nice for Jimmy, eh? Any port in a storm?"

"Exactly, oh, and I thought maybe you'd remember how I interceded when Deeming put the frighteners on you, when he was going to move you out and take over the joint. I didn't ask any favours then, but you knew the day might come. Well this is the day, and here I am."

Vella nodded, then he wiped a claw like hand over his face and took up the negatives.

"You going to wait? I can fix up a cot."

Danby walked towards the door, turning as he opened it, smiling down at the man.

"I'll be back at seven, the light wasn't good and it's shot through glass, do a good job, Jimmy, you'll get your reward on the other side."

"You reckon? I'll telephone my omm and give her the good news."

"Do it after you've developed the film, time's pressing." Danby closed the door and walked at speed down the stairway and onto the street. The rain had stopped and Piccadilly was humming with life. Danby walked along Shaftsbury Avenue turning left onto Frith Street. He thought about stopping for a drink as he passed the Dog and Duck, but thinking better of it he walked back to Old Compton Street and bought a bottle of Paddy from the little market there and hailed a taxi. He got dropped off at Marble Arch, letting the taxi move off before walking into Bayswater. The same man was sitting at his station; he stood as Danby entered, causing him to offer an acknowledgement.

"Pulling a late one?" Danby said, not pausing.
"How was it?"
"Come again?"
"The Benelux, any good?"
"Yes, sorry, yes it was fine."
"Me paper?"
"Paper?"
"Me Mail, you was going to drop it back to me."
"Yes, right, of course. You weren't here when I came down, sorry. I'm afraid I took it out with me, must have left it at the Benelux."
"I hadn't read it, I said."
"You did, you did say, well I'm sorry."
Danby reached into his pocket at put half a crown on the desk. Then he turned and headed up the stairs. When he got into his room he took up the newspaper, folded it and slid it into his coat pocket. Then he undressed and climbed between the sheets. He was asleep in moments. He'd meant to ask to be woken at six, but knew now that he'd need to be long gone by cockcrow.

Rake collected his whisky and Deakin's vodka and joined the little man at a corner table by the fire. The Mitre was busy, the atmosphere strikingly different from the West End bars that both men usually frequented, with cliques of men and very few women to be seen.

"It's like mausoleum in here," Rake said.
"Is it?"

"Feels like a golf club."
"I wouldn't know."
"You in a mood, John?"
"No."
"I've been thinking about Danby, why he wanted the negatives, what do you think?"
"You're the copper."
"I'm interested, come on, what do you reckon?"
"I have no idea. All I know is that my insurance policy, for what it was worth, has gone. I'm stranded aren't I? If I wasn't I wouldn't have frozen my pretty little derriere off for you, he's going to kill me."
"Keep your voice down."
"Why should I? He did for Bender and you know it."
Rake sat back and took a sip of his drink. Deakin downed his vodka and proffered the glass to Rake. Rake went back to the bar, keeping a weather eye on Deakin lest he escape. When he sat back down he laid his hand on Deakin's wrist.
"Drink up and settle down. We're going to visit Fry and you need to be calm."
"I am calm."
"I need you focused, I want you to listen out for any discrepancy, anything off in his story. You don't have to say anything; in fact I don't want you to say anything, all right? "
"Be a dummy you mean? I can do that."
"You can stay at my place tonight, we'll have a debrief and I'll bung in a score in the morning and you can move on. Go back down to Brighton, have a few nights at the Ship."
"I thought your flat was out of bounds for the likes of me."
"Things have changed."
"Changed how?"
Rake got up, Deakin drunk off his vodka and followed him through the door and onto Church End. They walked in silence to the house and Rake rang the buzzer for Fry's flat. They waited. The hall light came on and a very tall, slim figure opened the door.
"Phillip Fry?" Rake enquired.

"Chief Inspector Rake? Annie gave me your card, I did ring but got no response, and who is this?"

Deakin stepped into the light; Rake saw that Fry was surprised and not a little displeased.

"John Deakin, John – hello, why what a pleasure, do come in, come in. Most welcome, follow on; I'm on the very top floor under the eves. It's rather bijou but quite cosy."

They followed Fry along the passage and up three flights of narrow stairs to a door, which hung fully open. Rake could smell incense burning from the small landing and as they entered the living room he was struck by the wonder of the tiny space. It had clearly been servants quarters when the house was a family dwelling, and the fireplace had been opened up, with logs burning happily in the grate, giving out a wonderful glimmer, seeming anachronistic somehow, Edwardian almost and completely unexpected. The room was lit by the flickering glow of the fire and by myriad candles set along the mantelpiece and on a small North African brass topped circular table, the wax dripping unencumbered onto its surface. The shelving was full of leather bound volumes interspersed with antiquities that left Rake wishing he had the time to enquire as to their provenance. On the walls hung small paintings and sketches, one he knew to be a Nicholson and perhaps there was a compact oil by Stanley Spencer, a self portrait he was sure. On the wall above a two seat leather sofa hung a kilim, probably Turkish or even Persian, god, he thought, Ruth would love this. Fry took a book from the seat of an armchair by the fire and sat down. He clicked on a small reading lamp and bade his visitors to take the sofa.

"It's nice to see you again John – though I'm left wondering as to your presence. I'm guessing this is an informal visit?"

Deakin looked to Rake, but kept his counsel as agreed. Suddenly Fry leaped from his seat giving out an embarrassed, abrupt laugh, which caused Deakin to jump.

"I'm forgetting my manners, please excuse me. Now, what would you like to drink, can you drink Inspector, when on duty? I suppose not. John, what would you like?"

"What have you got?" Deakin asked.

"Oh, let's see," Fry walked over to a sideboard on which sat a silver-plated tray with several bottles on display. "Vermouth, gin, vodka, I could make you a very dry martini."

"All right, sounds good," Deakin said.

"Make it two, please Mister Fry. I'm going off duty after this."

"Phillip, please. Two dry martini's coming up."

As Fry busied himself with meticulous cocktail making, Rake took a moment to fully take in the ambience. He found it impossible to equate this urbane, pleasant fellow with the photograph that Sweet had shown him in an old copy of Picture Post. In the photo, which was from nineteen fifty seven Rake remembered, Fry was dressed in black leather trousers and a black silk blouson, open to display a narrow hairless chest. His sandy hair was dyed black and swept back in a greasy quiff, though it might have been a wig – Fry's hair being thin and wispy, Rake noticed. Fry handed drinks to his guests and sat down.

"Well then?" he said.

"Right," said Rake. "You probably know that I've visited most of the people present at the party in Tangier, November past."

"No, I didn't know."

"None of your friends got in touch, gave you the nod?"

"They're not my friends."

"Oh?"

"Are your colleagues your friends, Chief Inspector?"

"He hasn't got any friends, Phil," chipped in Deakin.

"Phillip."

"He hasn't got any friends, *Phillip*," Deakin said grimly.

"I haven't seen or heard from anyone since that dreadful night. I presume we're talking about Roy Huff?"

"Actually I'm particularly interested in Logan Frazer. It's still an open case."

"Now that was a surprise, I thought he'd died by fire, the immolated impresario I read somewhere, or perhaps not, I might have just thought it up myself in a dream, it happens sometimes. What made you think it was murder?"

154

"When they did the second post mortem examination they realised that there was no smoke in his lungs, so he clearly died before the fire was set. Then they re-examined the contusions and it became conclusive."

"Very shoddy work by the first pathologist, no? Was it a conspiracy do you think?"

"I'm just investigating the murder, Phillip, that's my remit, at the moment."

"And do you think the killer was one of the people at the party?"

"I certainly hold it as a possibility."

"Motive?"

"There must *be* a motive."

"Do you feel that it might be associated with the death of little Roy?"

"It might be, what do you think?"

"Oh now Mister Rake, I don't think anything at all. I honestly felt nothing when Roy died and I felt nothing when Logan died, whether or not it was murder. When I peeled Johnny Rocket from my skin the process of ecdysis was truly cleansing, purifying in fact. It's as though I was lifted from purgatory, and I felt, I *feel* divorced from those people and that time. You know, Mister Rake, I was surrounded by leeches and lepers for three years, you have no idea. The things I saw, heard – was part of. Oh, you can't imagine, corrosive would be an apt description."

"When did you stop being Johnny Rocket?"

"I was never Johnny Rocket."

"How do you mean?"

"I am, I *was* – a bass baritone, quite accomplished, though I say it myself. Frazer Logan heard me sing in Iolanthe at the Savoy. He was taken with me and said that he could make me a star. It was a Faustian pact of course, but I was young single and very naïve, so I leapt at it, sold my soul and took the filthy lucre, and by god Mister Rake, the lucre was foul. This was January fifty seven. He had me drag up as a rocker, you know, Ace café, ton ups along the Great North Road – can you imagine? But it worked, for a while, I had two big hits and then of course the strain began to show, my Doppelganger was so alien, the dissonance a chasm, I became really quite unwell, quite unwell. Cognac and amphetamines, not a diet I would recommend. I asked to be released from my contract in October last year, the Tangier debacle was the price of my freedom."

"Tell me about that night, the night Roy Huff died."

"What exactly do you want to know?"

"Start at the beginning."

"Well all right, so Logan told us that we were to attend a party at Barbara Hutton's palace in Tangier, this was November as you know. I didn't want to go, but in the end he agreed to let me out of my contract if I joined the expedition, so of course I capitulated. Charlie was there, and little Roy with the idiot savant Maurice, oh and Patrick Gupta of course, the fakir of Finsbury Park. We stayed at the Hotel Continental in the Medina, lovely for Charlie, what with all the kif floating about and the pretty boys."

"There was a gathering in the bar, before you went to the party. Some other people were there."

"That's right - John, of course showed up. Larry Parnes was there with Logan himself, and Noel Deeming for some reason."

"You know Deeming?"

"Only from the papers, he was being sought by you lot recently wasn't he? I didn't know who he was back then. He just sat there not saying anything, like the ghost at the feast. Horrible man, sweating in his serge suit with his comb over, nasty pudding of a man, I thought. Anyway, there was something clearly going on, whisperings and looks, I was glad to get out of there."

"You, Charlie Goole, Maurice Cohen and Patrick Gupta went to the palace."

"We did, and Larry Parnes – we all tootled off in a petite private hire bus."

"But not Frazer or Deeming?"

"No, not Frazer or Deeming."

"Why do you think Roy Huff didn't go with you?"

"He became unwell, John – you weren't at the party were you? I didn't see you there."

"We won't worry about that now," said Rake. "Carry on."

"Well we went, it was ghastly, we came back to find that Roy was dead and all hell broke loose."

"What kind of hell?"

"Maurice, he went berserk, went mad at Logan, threatening Armageddon, have you met Maurice? He's a Neanderthal, I wouldn't be surprised, well I wouldn't."

"Surprised at?"

"Never mind."

"Was Deeming there, when you returned?"

"They must have been there, I suppose. But to be honest I went to my room. I travelled home the next morning and I haven't seen them since, any of them."

"Did you go to the party as yourself or as Johnny Rocket?"

"He went."

"Sorry?"

"He went, the other one."

"You mean Johnny Rocket?"

"Yes, we all went in character."

"Were you surprised that Logan Frazer didn't attend the party?"

"I didn't give it a moments thought. Clearly there was something going on, some kind of subterfuge, it was tiresome really, and I rose above it. I had to get changed for the party of course, and it takes me quite some time, not only to put on the outer skin, but also to pull the viscera from where it dwells. It's a metamorphic process, Chief Inspector. So I went to my room and left them in the bar."

"Were you sharing a room?"

"Yes."

"Who with?"

"Johnny Rocket."

Rake's eyebrows lifted involuntarily and he looked across at Deakin, who was smirking horribly, enjoying the strangeness of the situation, recognising in Fry a manifest instability and relishing it. Rake had a sense that, why Johnny Rocket was a fiction, this manifestation of Fry as a sophisticated bohemian was just as fallacious, an over reaching attempt to become

157

someone who he thought he should be, would have been, if he'd trodden a different path.

"I wonder, Phillip, could I trouble you for another martini? You mix a superb cocktail."

"Me too, ducky," said Deakin proffering his glass. "Superb!"

Fry smiled and taking their glasses he went back to the tray and began mixing the drinks. Deakin caught Rake's eye and shook his head. Rake raised a quizzical brow and Deakin mouthed a few words that Rake couldn't decipher, then Fry turned round carrying the drinks.

"Have I missed something?" he said.

"John was just asking where the lavatory might be."

"One flight down, you'll find it next to the fire bucket." Deakin grunted and walked towards the door, collecting his glass from Fry as he headed out onto the landing.

"How do you know John, Mister Rake?" Fry said, handing Rake his drink and settling himself back in the chair.

"Just from the investigation. I had a meeting with him locally, about the case, and he wanted to say hello."

"He's a horrible little man, don't you think?"

"I don't sit in judgement."

"Oh, but you do, you strike me as being highly judgemental. It's a tool of your trade, surely? You've been judging me - my character, and my personality – whether or not I'm a reliable narrator. What conclusions have you reached, may I ask?"

"I would say that you are a rather unreliable narrator, Mister Fry," Rake finished his drink and stood. "I'll go and make sure that John hasn't purloined your toilet paper. Thank you for the drink and for your hospitality. I will be in touch."

"Do hurry back, it's been a pleasure. Oh, and kindly ask him to leave the glass on the stairs, you'll see yourself out?"

"Of course. Good night."

"Good night Mister Rake. Safe journey home."

Rake walked swiftly down to the lower landing, where he found Deakin smoking a cigarette. They walked together back towards the station.

158

"And?" Rake asked.

"He was lying, Frazer told me he was dumping Johnny Rocket, he said so in Tangier, in the hotel. And later I was there when Fry was pleading with him not to let him go."

"But I thought he had a couple of big selling records."

"That was at the beginning. Frazer said he'd gone off the boil, and that he was too mental to control, which he is, he's a loon."

Rake nodded thoughtfully. People were coming out of the Bell, and Rake realised it was closing time. He realised too that he wanted a proper drink, a drink, a smoke and a good think. He'd have to wait.

## Chapter Fourteen

Danby awoke from a dream at five the following morning. He lay for some moments trying to recollect the dream, because it had left him sweating, despite the chill. Frank Hanley had been trying to tell him something, but his mouth was full of blood. Bubbles of blood had escaped as he spoke, each popping in turn and as they burst a single word had become legible. Something like: She – Couldn't – Be – Heard –So – She – Smuggled – Her – Words – Upon – A – Yawn. As he came into full wakefulness, the dream evaporated and left him completely, apart from the imagined vision of Frank in his death throes. He climbed out of the bed, stretching kinks from his spine. The mattress had been too soft and too sunken. He showered and shaved, then dressed in his soiled shirt and undergarments and got into his suit. Normally a snappy dresser the dishevelment left him feeling disarmed and vulnerable somehow, but he shook the feeling away and went down the stairs. The reception was empty and he could hear snoring coming from a room to the left of the desk, so he stepped lightly out onto the street and walked through the park and onto Piccadilly.

    Jimmy Vella was sitting behind his desk when Danby walked into the little office. He had two glasses of whisky and a very serious face ready to greet him. Danby sat, raised his glass in salute and raised his eyebrows with the question. Vella nodded and flipped an envelope across the desk.

    "Churning, eh ghost? Fucking orribbli, right habib? That's one favour delivered, not to be repeated, okay?"

    Danby nodded and opened the envelope. He fanned the photographs as he might a deck of cards and studied the images. Although the room had only been lit by one overhanging bulb, and despite Deakin having shot through glass without a flash, the pictures seemed clear enough to identify Deeming, and the rape of a young male but, he feared, only if one had prior information. Roy Huff seemed not to be a participant, but more of an object, his pale flesh inert as if in death. It was like a Muybridge sequence, Deakin had used fast speed black and white 35mm film, and he'd achieved as clear an image as possible. Vella turned away and paced the room, avoiding Danby and the photographs.

"Could you make out what was going on?" Danby asked.

"Pervertit, that Deeming. Man, I seen a lot, I seen it all, but no – give me nightmares when I sleep, right? Right ghost? Fucking pig."

"Yes, of course, but would you have known, who and what?"

"I did the job, ghost, I didn't study with the microscope."

There were two sets of prints as promised. Danby asked for a second envelope and placed one set and the negatives in the envelope and addressed it to Duncan Webb care of The People.

"Can you drop this in by hand, Jimmy? Give it to Webb in person and do it yourself, you can ring through beforehand to make sure he's in or set up a rendezvous."

"Sure, what you going to do with the rest?"

"I know a copper might be interested."

Danby put the second set of prints in the original envelope, licked it, sealed it and addressed it to Chief Inspector Rake.

He walked to the Charing Cross Road and along the alley to the door that led to Rake's room. He rang the bell and then walked back to the street and looked up at the window. The light came on and he saw Rake look down. Danby walked back to the door and shortly it was opened by Rake.

"Late night?" Danby said.

"What do you want?"

"I want to come in."

"I've got to go to the station. You can come with me."

Danby reached into his coat pocket, Rake started and stepped back defensively. Danby grinned and produced the envelope.

"Little present."

"What is it?"

"Take a look."

Rake took the envelope, opened it and pulled out a photograph. He looked back at Danby, then took another image and held it under the bare light bulb that hung from the high ceiling. He

161

stepped back, leaving the door open and Danby followed him up the stairs.

He was surprised to see Deakin sprawled on the sofa, sound asleep, but he chose not to comment. Rake sat at the little table and looked through the photographs, his brow darkening with each one.

"You knew he'd done it, right?"

"Knowing and seeing are two different things."

"Is it enough?"

"I don't know, I recognise Deeming because I've met him, but you can't see enough of the boy to identify him."

"There are witnesses that they were together in Tangier."

"The room is anonymous, it could be a hotel room in any town in any country at any time."

"What about him?" Danby said, indicating Deakin. "He took the fucking pictures, he knows."

"He's scared of Deeming, and it could open him up to a blackmail charge."

"Subpoena the little cunt, Jesus, this is pathetic. Anyway, whoever it is it's illegal, and you can see it's a kid."

"Maybe, it's something, I'm not arguing with that, I'm just being honest, and he's got a damn good brief."

"Well fuck it, I've sent the photographs and negatives to the papers, it'll set the cat among the pigeons."

"You damn fool, it'll be prejudicial to any prosecution. You've got to get them back."

Danby laughed humourlessly and shook his head. Deakin stirred and rolled over, blinking in bewilderment at the scene unravelling before him.

"One way or the other, Deeming is fucked, I've stitched him up proper. I don't just want him locked up, I want him skewered, hung drawn and quartered. I don't want him being daddy on the wing, Rake. See I want him with the nonces, with the kiddie fiddlers and the rapists, kept in isolation for years. Looking over his shoulder inside and on the out. He'll be the walking dead and then one day he'll get got."

Rake put the photographs in the envelope and stood. He walked to where his jacket hung on a door hook and slipped the envelope into an inside pocket. Then he shrugged on the jacket and ran a hand through his hair. Lifting his collar he looped a tie around his throat and then he stood looking at Danby thoughtfully.

"I'm arresting you for the shooting of two people at the Marylebone Yacht Club, you do not have to say anything…"

"Oh for fuck's sake, Rake." Danby almost laughed, but suddenly his face hardened and his eyes darkened perceptibly. Rake saw for the first time the man he was dealing with, it brought him up short, but only for the briefest moment.

"But anything you do say will be taken down and may be used…"

"You're being ridiculous."

"In evidence against you. Are you going to come of your own free will or do I need these?" Rake brought out a pair of handcuffs.

"You want to try putting those on me, copper?"

"No." said Rake, and he ran his fingers through one cuff and swung a perfect arc, up from his waist, hitting Danby on the chin and following through beautifully. Danby fell back into the table, upending it and crashing to the floor. He struggled to his feet, reaching for the Webley but Rake kicked it out of his hand. Danby rose to his feet, lacing the knuckle-dusters through his fingers and the two men faced off, stalking one another in the compact space. Deakin reached down from the sofa and picked up the revolver. He pointed it at Danby.

"Don't!" Rake commanded, and in that instant, as his eyes were drawn toward Deakin, Danby hit him hard across the temple. Rake stumbled, almost fell, his knees buckling – and Danby was out of the door and heading noisily down the stairs. Groaning, Rake straightened and ran to the landing as the front door slammed. He tried to run down the stairs after the fugitive, but his legs were like rubber, failing him. Frustrated, he sat on a step and took in a deep breath, exhaling on an oath. Deakin stood on the landing, looking down, the gun in his hand. The neighbour's door opened and an old man shuffled onto the landing, taking in the spectral image of this emaciated figure, his genitals clearly visible under a stained grey singlet.

"What on earth?" he said.

"And you can fuck off cunty," Deakin hollered.

"I'll be reporting this to the police."

"He is the police," said Deakin, pointing down at the detective with the barrel of the revolver.

"I'm reporting this, I'm reporting it to the Chief Constable."

"You can report it to MI fucking five you old bollocks, and good luck!"

Rake shouted up from the stairwell for Deakin to be quiet and the old man closed his door with some muffled admonition that Deakin could not decipher. Rake looked at his watch, it was eight forty three. He was due for a show down with Harper at nine; he wasn't going to make it. He could feel his temple throbbing and an egg-sized lump was beginning to mass there. But he had the photographs and he had Deakin, if he could persuade him to underpin his hypothesis with facts.

Danby spat blood onto the Charing Cross Road as he walked swiftly back to Piccadilly. He climbed the stairs of the Eros cinema and entered Jimmy Vella's office without knocking. Vella looked up startled.

"Back already? Christ and Moses, give me a chance! I'm meeting Webb at twelve thirty at The Moka-ris, okay? "

"Okay, good. Pass me some paper."

"What's up, you don't look too tasty?"

"It's nothing, look Jimmy, I need a passport, bogus, and I need it quick, as in tomorrow." Danby made several quick notes, asked for an envelope, addressed it to Webb and sealed it.

"You've had your favour, ghost – you're pushing your luck."

"No, Jimmy – I can pay, but it's got to be now."

"It'll cost."

"How much?"

"Maybe two ton, maybe more."

"Really? I can cover one fifty."

164

Jimmy Vella made a noise in his throat and plastered a sad, helpless expression across his face. Then he shrugged and turned his hands palm upward in a gesture familiar to Danby.

"One fifty and my Rolex, and that's that."

Vella clicked his fingers and Danby handed over the watch. It was a gold Rolex 3362 which Danby had stolen in nineteen forty-seven, a smash and grab raid in The Burlington Arcade.

"Okay, good. But it will take two days, at least. I got to contract out. But you come with me and I'll do the snap. You got the dosh?"

"Seventy five now and the rest C.O.D, you can hang on to the watch. "

Danby counted out the money and slapped it on the desk. Vella picked up the notes and counted them carefully.

"Don't you trust me, Jimmy?"

Vella chuckled. Danby joined in. Then both men walked down a flight to the studio. Danby handed Vella the envelope.

"Give it to Webb along with the photographs."

"Anything I should know?"

"You can read about it in the paper on Sunday."

"I don't read the papers, ghost. I'm happier being ignorant."

Danby shrugged and took a seat while Vella set up the lights and loaded the camera.

When Rake walked into Harper's office it was approaching nine forty five and the old man was seething. Then he looked at Rake's face and his brow knitted with something like concern. He pointed to the chair and Rake sat.

"I'm sorry I'm so late boss, something came up."

"I can see that, what happened?"

"I tried to arrest Danby, it didn't work out." Rake took the Webley from his coat and laid it upon the desk. "I took this from him, it hasn't been fired. Look I've got John Deakin outside, he's willing to talk, but only to you at this stage."

"This is all very irregular, Rake."

"You should hear what Deakin has to say, sir."

"You know Rake, I've read the report. Deeming suggests that you and this Deakin fellow were or are," he hesitated, "intimate."

"I know."

"Well?"

"Sir, it's not true. I shielded Deakin, unwisely I know, but I did. He was in fear of his life and it was an error of judgement in hindsight, but at the time I made a decision and prioritized his safety, I don't regret it."

"You could have brought him in."

"He wouldn't have come in."

"You had options."

"I can't argue with you, sir."

"I am going to have to suspend you from duty, I've sent a memorandum to the Deputy Chief Constable. You will receive a formal letter in due course."

Rake nodded. Harper poured a glass of water and handed it across the desk. Rake took a sip and carefully placed the glass down.

"Will you please take a look at these photographs? I should warn you, they are extremely unpleasant." He passed the envelope to Harper and looked down at his lap. Two long minutes passed, the only sound was something like the shuffling of a deck of cards.

"So? I'm listening."

"Perhaps I could bring Deakin in now, sir. He took those pictures."

Harper pressed the intercom and instructed his assistant to show Deakin into the office. Deakin ambled in, looking like a Bantam Cock, all bravado and front, doing all he could to create an impression of nonchalance. He pointed to a seat, Harper nodded, and he pulled it noisily away from the desk and sat, looking around the room.

"Nice," he said, stretching out his little legs, making himself at home. "I'm doing him a favour, coming in. I just want you to know that. He's a fine policeman and a good bloke. Saved my fucking life, right? I'm here to do my civic duty, you can write that down."

Harper was unimpressed, and it showed clearly on his thin, dour face.

"Well, what am I looking at?"

Rake nodded at Deakin, encouraging him to elucidate. He didn't need much motivation.

"That's Noel Deeming tupping a lad called Rot Huff in the Hotel Continental, Tangier last November. Roy Huff was a singer, went by Little Mickey Magnet. He was sixteen and Deeming and Logan Frazer got him drugged up and sloshed so that Deeming could have his wicked way with the kid who, by the way, took his own life later that night."

"And you know all this how? Be specific please Mister Deakin."

"Logan Frazer paid me to take the photographs. I was supposed to give them and the negatives to Frazer, but somehow I didn't get round to it and then he got murdered, so I kept them for a while, then I moved the photos on to an acquaintance, though I kept the negs, for insurance."

"Insurance against what?"

"Being murdered by Noel Deeming."

" To whom did you give the photographs?"

"H.H. Bender, he got murdered too, at the Blackheath Golf Club. That was Deeming, obviously. Old H.H. was putting the screws on him."

"As you know, sir," Rake interjected, "I pulled Deeming in for the Frazer murder. He had an alibi, cast iron, he was in Spain with John Lambert, I've spoken to Mister Lambert and he confirms that Deeming was holidaying with him and his wife throughout the period that Frazer was killed."

"What about Bender?"

"So far we have no evidence beyond hearsay that Deeming had any motive for killing Bender."

"It's not fucking hearsay is it, Rakey? I'm here saying it quite blatantly. H.H. was blackmailing Deeming, that's why he wanted the photographs."

"Frazer owed Deeming money, a lot of money apparently," said Rake. "Frazer set the boy up as payment or part payment of the debt."

"That's right, Frazer told me, he said the kid was a deposit, paying off the interest."

Harper swivelled his chair towards Rake, effectively cutting Deakin out of the conversation for the moment.

"We'll give Deeming a tug," said Harper. Deakin spluttered a coughing guffaw, until Harper's look shut him up. "It'll have to be Sweet, you're out Rake, I'm sorry. Just go home – you," he pointed at Deakin, " will be catered for here."

"Oh really? I should coco, absolutely no," Deakin said, sitting up straight for the first time.

"You will be accommodated in a custody suite with round the clock protection until further notice. Either that, Mister Deakin, or I will be forced to have you detained under a charge, or in this case, charges. It's up to you."

"I'm a friendly witness, your honour!"

"I can see charges pending: aiding in the corruption of a minor, conspiracy, blackmail, withholding evidence – do I need to go on? I didn't think so. "

Deakin looked pathetically at Rake, who was now standing and heading towards the door. Rake felt like a heel, but really, what else could he have don e?

Noel Deeming awoke at nine thirty on Sunday 20th of February and called out for Danieli who had slept on the couch for the past couple of nights. There was no answer and he swore under a grunted breath as he swung himself out of bed. He looked down at his swollen, varicose legs and felt immediately gloomy. Standing he dragged his dressing gown from the foot of the bed and padded into the en-suite. The man looking back at him from the mirror was oedematous, jowly and bleary eyed. He turned on the hot tap and splashed water onto his face, and then he ran a comb under the faucet and dragged it through his hair. He looked once again at his reflection.

"Cunt," he said to himself. He leaned, stiff limbed against the sink. He turned and tried to urinate, farting repeatedly as he strained, finally he sat and managed to piss. His penis burned and he couldn't produce a steady flow. He thought about Vernon and a rising anger began to glow behind his eyes. He wiped a toilet tissue across the glans and sniffed it. Then he dropped it into the bowl, flushed the chain and carefully washed his hands. He walked through the bedroom and into the lounge. The couch was empty, a sheet and eiderdown flung to the floor and the cushions set akimbo at one end. Disgraceful, he thought to himself, Danieli knew the pack drill; tidy up you greasy fucker Deeming thought, but he might have said it aloud, he wasn't sure. Then he saw the paper, left open on the coffee table. Now he was furious, Danieli knew, *everyone* knew not to touch the papers until Deeming had finished with them. Muttering, Deeming took the paper into the kitchen and placed it on the Formica surface of the table. He boiled the kettle and made a strong pot of tea. Two sugars, milk in first, brew for ten minutes, like his old mum decreed. He took his cup to the table and turned to the first page.

### The Photo We Just Cant Print!
### The Pop Star and the Gangster exclusive
### Wild nights in Tangier hotspot: Police Probe
### notorious West End villain after tragic suicide of teen idol

Deeming read on, it was over bar the shouting. All there, laid out in fascinating innuendo. No names, but the promise of more to come including statements from others present and the possibility of links to other crimes including the murder of a prominent figure in the world of entertainment. Danieli had known, of course, had known it was him as soon as he read the article, and he'd scarpered. They'd all scarper now. Rats leaving a sinking ship, rats, rats – useless turncoats. He saw that his digits were drumming on the Formica; his eyes were wide and staring at, staring at – at nothing. The room had disappeared. His mouth was open, wide – swallowing everything, his whole world was stuck in his gullet and suddenly, and without warning he vomited it up, soaking the newspaper. He upended the Formica table, whirling he raged, completely outside of himself. Finally he wept, finally he called out for his mother, and finally he sank back onto the chair, hearing the words, knowing it all - all at once. *I'll strip you naked in front of the world.*

"Danby!" he heard himself say. He tried to read the article again, through the kaleidoscopic mess. There was no mention of

H.H. Bender. Not yet anyway. So, all right, Danieli was on the lam, but that left Vernon. Vernon would betray him, he might even give himself up and turn Queens evidence before he warrants were issued. He was milky, and he'd probably given Deeming a dose, diseased little toe-rag. Deeming started to feel better; he always felt better when he had a plan, and he always felt better when he was angry. Anger fills all the holes where pain might dwell, his old lady had said, wise old tart.

Danby borrowed a small holdall from Jimmy Vella and walked to Bourne and Hollingsworth on Oxford Street. He stole a shirt, a sports jacket and a pair of trousers and left the store wearing the ensemble, his soiled clothing stuffed into the holdall. Then he went into Burtons and bought underwear and socks and a rather nice red cashmere scarf. Finally he bought a toothbrush, toothpaste and shaving kit in Boots and headed to Oxford Circus Tube, taking the east bound Central Line to Mile End. He found a seedy little guesthouse on Eric Street and booked in as Mister Leonard Temple, settling in for a well deserved catnap before walking the short distance to Ropery Street. Vernon lived in a bedsitting room on the first floor front of a building above a small auto repair shop where he sometimes worked as a mechanic. The Magnette was parked in Lockhart Street, just a few doors along from Vernon's hovel. It being a Sunday, Danby knew that the lad would not be working, so he leant against a wall and smoked a couple of cigarettes, waiting for it to get dark. At five fifteen he saw a light go on in Vernon's window. He flicked his cigarette into the street and walked across the road to the house. There was only one bell so he picked up a handful of gravel from the patch of garden and flung it up at the window. The net curtains were pulled back and Vernon's face pressed up against the glass looking down. When he saw whom it was he darted back, so Danby picked up a heavier pebble and threw it more forcefully. The windowpane cracked, or sounded like it cracked, in any event Vernon reappeared and signalled open palmed for Danby to wait. A minute later Danby heard footsteps clumping down the stairs, the hall light came on and the door opened. Vernon poked his head out looking both ways along the street, and then he opened the door wider and stepped onto the path.

Vernon was an extremely good looking fellow of twenty three or twenty four. Though more handsome that Alfie Atkins, Vernon was effeminate, tall and slender and delicate, Deeming preferred Alfie, who was muscular and pugnacious. Alfie was a couple of years younger than Vernon, but seemed much younger, a youth in fact, and most tellingly he wasn't homosexual. But Alfie was long gone, and Deeming always turned to Vernon as a substitute driver, gofer and plaything when Alfie wasn't around.

"Hello Mister Danby, what's up?"

"What do you think might be up, Vernon?"

Vernon shrugged and took another look up and down the street. Danby mirrored him, and then shook his head.

"No, just you me and them there chickens. You going to invite me in?"

Danby brushed past the boy and climbed the stairs. The small bedsitting room was sparse and dishevelled, smelling of Old Spice, tobacco and reefer. So, Vernon was a viper, Danby noted the rolling papers and the coiled lid of a cigarette packet in the ashtray. Vernon followed him into the room and stood awkwardly under the naked light bulb that hung in the centre of the high ceiling.

"Let's have a smoke, Vernon."

"You what?"

"Roll one up and let's share a smoke, for old time's sake. For the good old days, eh?"

Vernon shrugged and sat on the bed. He opened the drawer of a utility bedside cabinet, took out the makings and rolled a reefer. He lit the dovetail end, which flared momentarily, and then he took a long pull, exhaling blue/brown smoke up towards the nicotine ceiling. Tentatively, he handed the reefer to Danby, who sat beside him on the bed. They smoked in silence until the joint was dead. Danby ground the butt into the ashtray and exhaled mightily, some vestige of smoke escaping his lungs along with the breath. In the long silence that followed Danby could hear the ticking of Vernon's watch, he could hear the walls breathing, he could feel his exhaustion in a visceral and sudden depletion. He blew out his cheeks, as if he'd been on a long run. He'd been running all his life, and it wasn't the time to slow down now.

"You alright Mister Danby?"

"Well Vernon, I'll say this, things can only get better old son. I'll take a cigarette, if you don't mind."

Vernon fished out a pack of Senior Service and Danby nodded a thank you and lit up. He put his hand on Vernon's knee and squeezed.

"You don't look too good Mister Danby, honest."

"It's been a shit week, Vernon. You know I just realised how much I don't want to hurt you. It sort of clarified all of sudden in my head. Clear as crystal, solid as a rock. But the fact is, unfortunately, and this is how it's been going lately, I might have to hurt you very severely."

Danby increased his grip incrementally as he talked. Vernon gasped and arched back against the headboard.

"I might have to damage you Vernon. Unless you do what I need you to do."

"What? Tell me, what?"

"You ever heard of the Trojan horse?"

## Chapter Fifteen

At four thirty on the afternoon of Tuesday 22nd February Rake's phone rang. It was Sweet, keeping a promise against his own better judgement. It appeared that Noel Deeming had been interviewed at Paddington Green station under caution in connection with the rape of a teenage boy in November nineteen fifty nine. The photographs were not seen as material to the investigation as they were considered to be inconclusive. Due to the fact of Rake's suspension on misconduct charges, the case was not to be overseen by West End Central, so Sweet had had to collect on favours owed to get the gen on the interview.

"So?"

"What do you think?" Sweet asked, sounding tired.

"He was let out on bail?"

"He didn't go in front of the beak, spent a couple hours at the station then left threatening retribution via his brief.

"Whittaker?"

"Whittaker. Probably won't get to court. The story in Sunday's paper was recognised as being prejudicial to any prosecution. Deeming can't sue unless he's named, it would be an admission that he's in the frame, but they won't name him now, they can't unless he's brought before the court and convicted – even then, it won't be a scoop will it?"

"No, but Danby's been clever, cleverer than us, Peter. Deeming will be isolated now, vulnerable. Those old lags in his firm won't want to be associated with a kiddie rapist, and they'll know it was him. Well sod it Peter, maybe justice will run its course on the street."

"You don't mean that, boss."

"I'm not your boss Peter, and I do mean it. Deeming is a slippery venal bastard, and I hope he gets his. Look, I just want to say thank you, I appreciate it, Peter. I know you didn't want to do this and I probably didn't deserve your help, I'm not good at asking you know that, so." Rake ran out of words.

"You sound bitter, Cyril."

Rake placed the receiver in its cradle and tried to order his thinking. Then he put his old black Crombie on and headed onto the Charing Cross Road. He hailed a taxi and wended his way through heavy traffic towards Hendon.

Rake reached the house at five fifty. The skies had slowly darkened during the journey and the big old dwelling was well lit and looked welcoming. Rake thought that he should consider moving back to the suburbs, to a flat in a nice villa, somewhere like West Hampstead, somewhere warm and welcoming, with neighbours and parkland where he might wander through the seasons. He looked up at the top window, Fry's window. The candles were burning; he could see the light dancing behind the glass where the curtains hadn't been fully closed. He pressed the bell for flat number four and waited. No one came, so he tapped on the door. Presently the attractive neighbour opened the door, smiling prettily when she recognised the policeman.
"Hello again," he said.
"Oh, hello."
"He in?"
"He is, yes. I heard him earlier, walking up and down, and he's playing music again – he hasn't done that for a long time," she lowered her voice. "It's awfully loud, not like him at all."
Rake tilted his head and sure enough he could hear music coming from the top of the house. He thought he recognised the music as being Mozart, the Requiem in D Minor, though it was distorted through volume and distance, ricocheting around the stairwell, scratching at his ears.
"Shall I go up?" He pointed his index finger and she nodded and stepped aside. Rake went to doff his hat, but realised he'd left without it. He walked up the stairs to Flat 4 and tapped on the door, he got no answer, so carefully he pushed the door open. Candles and the fire lighted the room, with incense burning in a Chinese lion dog censer on the crowded mantle, and another smell, an undertone of burnt syrup or something like it. Philip Fry was lying on the floor, his head propped on a Turkish cushion. He was clothed in black, as Rake had seen in the old photograph in Picture Post that Peter Sweet had shown him. Pointed black boots, tight black trousers and a shiny black shirt; satin perhaps, Rake wasn't sure. Fry's thin sandy hair had been

slicked back and dyed, with boot polish by the look of it. The record came to an end, the needle clicking before being ejected. Another disc flopped noisily onto the turntable and something choral began to reverberate through the small room.

Rake walked over to the hi-fi and turned it off, the music grinding to a slow fade. He looked down at Fry, or rather at Johnny Rocket, noticing the makeup that adorned his face, making him seem cadaverous, like a distempered skull. There was a pipe there on the rug, and a small charred bowl with a similarly blackened needle resting on the lip of the bowl. Fry didn't move or even open his eyes. Then his lips curled and a mid-Atlantic snarl escaped him.

"I knew you'd come back."

"May I sit?" Rake asked.

"Do as thou wilt."

"Do you know why I'm here?"

Rake sat on the small sofa and lit a Craven A. Then he stood and shrugged the Crombie from his shoulders and draped it over the arm of the seat. The room was stifling; the air heavy with incense and wood smoke and the strange, sweet tinge of opium. He sat once again and waited for a reply.

"Your timing is awful Chief Inspector, I am very tired and well, rather inebriated, if I'm honest."

"Well Mister Fry, I'm very tired too."

"The only horrible thing in the world is ennui."

"Oscar Wilde."

"Very good."

"But it isn't ennui, Mister Fry, I'm just exhausted."

"Perhaps you should be in bed."

"I can't sleep when something is niggling at me."

"Is something niggling at you?"

"Indeed."

"What, may I ask is niggling at you?"

"What's niggling at me, Mister Fry, is who killed Logan Frazer?"

"I can help you with that."

"I know."

175

A sickly smile spread across the gaunt face of the man lying prone on the floor, and one eye opened in something like a wink.

Deeming had telephoned Vernon at seven thirty on the evening of Tuesday 22nd February, summoning him to the Mayfair flat at nine that night. As promised, Vernon rang Danby at the guesthouse on Eric Street, and they arranged to meet outside Mile End tube station at eight fifteen. It was an unseasonably warm evening; a harbinger of spring, people were out in light clothing and Danby had forsaken his overcoat, carrying Erskine's Enfield .38 in his belt, hidden under the new jacket. He'd cleaned and serviced the revolver and he could smell lubricant on his fingers as he smoked. They hardly spoke on the journey, but as they passed Bruton Street Danby told Vernon to pull over. He climbed nimbly over the seat and shuffled onto the floor of the Magnette. Vernon pulled away from the kerb and drove into the car park of Deeming's building right on time.

    Vernon pressed his palm to the horn and stuttered a greeting. Deeming appeared at his window in acknowledgement. Vernon drove into the designated space and switched the engine off.

    "Give it a minute," Danby commanded. "Has he gone?"

    "Yes, he'll have gone to the entry phone."

Danby climbed out of the Magnette and passed by the blackened oily silhouette of the Daimler. He walked swiftly to the door, pressing the buzzer as instructed: ...- Morse code for the letter V, Vernon not being gifted with a key to the apartment. The door hummed and clicked and Danby pushed it open and entered the hallway. He walked up the stairs to the penthouse. Taking the revolver from his waistband he tapped on the door. Deeming was in his dressing gown and slippers, freshly barbered and powdered, smelling of Aqua Velva, his smug expression turning to bewilderment as Danby pushed his way into the apartment, the revolver pointing at Deeming's forehead.

    "Hello poncey," he said, backing Deeming into the big armchair. "Cover yourself up, I'm not here to fuck you, you're already fucked. Empty your pockets, inside out."

Deeming did as he was told, producing only a handkerchief. Then Danby went swiftly through the flat. Finding it unoccupied he sat on the sofa and crossed his legs, making himself comfortable.

"All your little pals deserted you then, eh? They'll be taking over, what? Poncey? They'll have a little cabal set up by now, eh? They've probably been planning it for weeks, must've seen the signs, eh boss? You reckon? What was it you used to say: Money rolls up hill, shit rolls down, that was it, what? Money and shit, well – what do you reckon now, Noel? " Danby leaned forward, the gun hanging limply in his hand, his eyes focused on Deeming's, trying to look past the man's bland expression. "Can I call you Noel? You can call me Harry if you like, for old times sake."

"Smug ain't you?"
Deeming held his erstwhile friends gaze, looking quite comfortable, quite relaxed now. He pulled his gown demurely across his bloated body and stood. He went to the drinks trolley and poured himself a large cognac, not offering one to Danby. Then he sat back down, drew in the aroma and sipped at the liquor.

"Are you here to murder me, Harry?"

"Well, Noel, that's an interesting question isn't it? It's like, am I here to put you out of your misery, or am I here to experience your misery with you? Voyeuristically I mean, to get the most out of it, you know - squeeze the juice out of it. Just knowing isn't always enough, is it? I mean, is it? Look, honestly, if we're *being* honest Noel, someone is going to kill you soon anyway, we both know that, either in the nick when you get sent down, or on the out, if they get impatient. You will go down, sooner or later. That copper Rake has got you in his sights for one."

"He won't be a copper much longer, I marked his card for him, daft cunt."

"And then there's your mob, they'll hang you upside down from a lamppost like Mussolini, make it public, an expulsion, like a cleansing. Wait till they see the next instalment in the Sunday papers, I got it all down."

"I'm gagging the papers, you prat. Think I can't? It's done."
"Is it?"
"Easy, piece of piss."
"I think you over estimate yourself, Noel"
"It's a piece of *piss*!"
"And then there's H.H. Bender."
"Never heard of him."
"Never heard of old H.H.?"
"Never."
"Never?"
"I just said."
"Funny that."
"Funny, what like a joke?"
"Like a little fib. You're a little fat fibber, Noel."
"Prove it. He's your namesake, Harry, two little peas from the same pod. You won't go so quick, I can promise you that."
"Can you?"
"Stand on me, son. I give you my word."

Danby stood and walked to the drinks trolley, pouring a large whisky, swirling it in the glass and drinking appreciatively. He stood over Deeming, and then suddenly bending down, he brought his face closer to the man, breathing whisky and stale cigarettes.

"Expecting company?"
"Like you said, who would be coming?"

Danby walked back to the sofa and sat down crossing his legs, his right foot swinging easily, in time with a tune only he could hear.

"Vernon," he said.
"What about Vernon?"
"You gave him a key, this key," Danby produced a set of keys on a steel ring, he tossed them at Deeming, who winced. The keys dropped noiselessly onto the rug. "And you gave him a gun, this gun," he produced a Beretta 9mm Short from his inside jacket pocket and watched, smiling, as the blood drained from Deeming's doughy face. "After I met with Vernon on Sunday he rang you and together you came up with this little, what's it called, subterfuge. Once I got settled, thinking he didn't have a

key, he was supposed to come creeping in all subtle like and pop me in the back of my head. Only I was with him when he made the call, snuggled up close to him on his little bed in his horrible room and I heard it all. And together we came up with another proposition. This one, where you end up looking like a cunt and I end up with a full fucking house." Deeming's mouth opened and closed a few times, but no sound emerged.

"What? What – come on? You think I'm stupid, Noel? You've got a spy hole on your door mate, you knew it was me knocking, acting all surprised you berk. Guess what – Danieli didn't dump the knife you used on Bender, he told Vernon he's hidden it, just in case you turned on him. You think they watched you kebob that sad little man and didn't think you might just want to get rid of witnesses? Vernon knows he's on your list, he's not as daft as you think, it's survival, Noel. Sharpens the mind, gets the paranoia bubbling. You wanted to be feared; well now you are, like a rabid dog in a kinder garden. How's that working out for you?"

Deeming climbed slowly out of his seat. His breath wheezed shallowly, rising from the top of his lungs in short, sharp expulsions. His dressing gown slid open, exposing his heavy, flaccid genitalia and his huge distended belly. He walked stiffly to the window and looked down at the car park.

"He's gone, Noel. He's going to turn himself in before it's too late. He's going to tell them where the knife is hidden. He's going to tell them about Lenny Matta, he'll spill his guts for a deal, and he'll get a deal. What sort of deal do you think you'll be offered?" Danby dropped the Beretta back into his pocket and laid the .38 on the cushion, fishing out a cigarette and patting his trousers to find his lighter. "Sit down, make yourself comfortable, we're not going anywhere."

Deeming stayed at the window, his forehead pressed lightly on the frigid glass. His shoulders began to quiver, for the briefest moment Danby thought he might be crying, it was then that he felt the cold steel on the back of his head. Deeming turned towards him, he was laughing, a breathless cawing rising from the depths of his belly, sticking in his throat then erupting forth from his open mouth, filling the room, echoing around

Danby's brain. A slender hand reached down beside him and collected the .38 from the cushion. Danby craned his neck and looked up.

"Hello Vernon," he said.

The room was quiet now, save for the occasional metallic rattle in the grate as the wind pulled and pushed at the flue while the fire slowly waned. Rake waited patiently as Fry dozed, his jaw hanging loosely, making Rake think of Marley's ghost. The fire continued to die as the hour passed; it was approaching eight when Fry stirred, taking in a shuddering breath and expelling it through congested lungs.

"So then, Mister Fry, you wanted to help me," Rake offered, his voice sounding strange in this strange situation. Fry let out a throaty groan and sat up blinking. He shivered, or rather shuddered, and then he struggled to his feet and plonked himself down on the familiar chair. Fry fingered through the ashtray and came up with a dog end, which he lit, it flamed momentarily and then he drew deeply on the tobacco. When he spoke the transatlantic twang was gone, he was Fry again, in a Halloween costume.

"If you ask the right questions, I'll help you. The moment that you behave stupidly I'll close my mouth and I will not speak again."

"Fair enough. Why did Phillip Fry decide to kill Logan Frazer?"

"Very good, very astute a good punt as they say. But I am of course Philip Fry, I am fully cognizant of the fact of myself, holistically, I'm not fragmented I just have an alter ego, this," he wafted a limp hand along his sunken frame, "personage was a conceit dreamt up by Logan but it fitted, I found. It exorcised several demons that had been plaguing me since childhood. Johnny Rocket can do things, say things, react, behave in ways that I could never have imagined, and you see, Mister Rake, people responded, they liked him, for a while they adored him. They gave him money; they gave him love, unconditional love. They gave him their bodies, their mouths, their flesh, their - all. Little virgin nymphs lined up back stage, it was a teenage bacchanal honestly, you wouldn't believe it, the tightness, the wetness, the little pink parts, shiny pink parts."

Fry chuckled, phlegm jockeying in his throat, searching expectoration, he swallowed noisily. His eyes glinted in the candlelight, searching for a response in Rake's placid face.

"I liked being Johnny Rocket, who wouldn't? Wouldn't you? One has carte blanche to do whatever one can get away with and one has access to all the naughty potions that reinforce ones sense of anomie, of freedom, can you imagine? I found a taste for things that had previously only surfaced in my dreams. He was impervious, invulnerable, it was glorious."

"You have started to talk in the third person, Mister Fry. It won't wash, just a warning to you. Try your best not to do it."

Fry shifted in his seat. He started to poke at the ashtray again. Rake tossed him his packet of cigarettes and waited. Fry extracted a cigarette then threw the packet back, spinning it like a cardboard side plate, aggressively, with feeling. Rake caught it dexterously, which rather surprised both men. They sat and smoked in silence for a while. Fry's eyelids were getting heavy, so Rake spoke up.

"Talk me through the murder, Mister Fry. Start at the beginning of the day in question."

"It was Monday December the twenty first, a very cold day, very cold. In fact I was recovering from a dose of flu, it was about you may remember, so I was feeling it, the cold I mean. Logan had told me in November that he was letting me go, letting Johnny Rocket go, abandoning him. Too old you see, he said, too old. You're just too old, boy, he said. Look son, you're losing your looks, losing your hair, losing your teeth. With your shirt unbuttoned you look like a fucking carcass; he said that to me, those were his actual words, a fucking carcass. That was in the November. After Tangier he was consumed by Roy Huff's suicide, he took the phone off the hook and hibernated. I imagine he was feeling responsible, well, in a way I suppose he was wasn't he?

So eventually I summoned up the courage to go to his apartment in Kensington to have it out with him. I rang the doorbell, rang and rang the doorbell, but he didn't come down, so I waited for someone to go out and eventually a nice old lady left to take her poodle for a shit in Holland Park and in I slid. I banged on his door, I shouted in fact – caterwauled really, like a banshee. Eventually the door cracked an inch or so, I pushed and there was Logan, in his silk Kimono looking like Suzy Wong gone to the dogs. It was pitiful, Mister Rake, pitiful. Can I cadge another cigarette?"

Rake stood and offered a cigarette; Fry took one, gracefully this time. He lit it and inhaled deeply, expelling smoke from his nose and his mouth as he spoke.

"I was in a state of high arousal, Mister Rake. Not like myself at all. It was Johnny there in that room, that isn't an excuse; it's a simple statement of fact. I couldn't have faced him again, I'd already tried, you see? I'd tried to explain my dilemma, I'd pleaded and cajoled and begged. But this time I was angry, furious, in fact I was *incandescent.* Logan had given me fame, but he'd also fuelled the inferno with drugs and with sex and with money, and now he was sending me back into this untenanted," he wafted his hand once again, "thing that I am."

Fry was becoming agitated, living that moment, back there in that room with Logan Frazer and the knell of dismissal and the disintegration it foretold.

"I used Johnny, I put him on like an ill fitting suit, like I had done night after night to get up on stage and sing those ridiculous songs to those little bitches wetting the seats in every seedy dancehall and ballroom in every suburb from Neasden to Nantwich. He just sat there, shaking his head every now and then, bored probably, I mean fucking bored! I'd seen how he'd treated Kenny Muir, poor little Elmo Tweak, and all the other over the hill artistes, and I wasn't even offered that! I might have taken that, in the end, god forbid, but I might. Well, I wasn't, he offered me nothing, not even his sympathy."

"So you were being honest when you spoke about Roy Huff, about not caring about his suicide? I had thought, well I had thought that it was revenge."

Fry sunk back into the chair, his heavy lids seeming to want to close of their own volition, notwithstanding it seemed, his need to confess.

"I loved the boy, we all did really, except Kenny – but he hated everyone. Roy was a lovely chap, now he did have talent, and respect to him for what he did."

"He was sixteen."

"It doesn't matter, not in the end. He got tired of being used and he took control."

"Of his death, not of his life."

Fry nodded, he breathed deeply and rubbed his chest as if to soothe a palpitation. Rake looked at his watch, it was eight fifty. He'd asked Sweet to wait at the station until nine, though he thought the D.S. would sit it out. He shifted in his seat, leaning forward and speaking in his resonant, officious tone of voice.

"Before we proceed Mister Fry, I'm going to read you your rights, do you understand?" Fry nodded. "Phillip Fry, you do not have to say anything unless you wish to do so, but anything you do say will be taken down and may be given in evidence. I must also tell you, before we go any further, that I intend to contact my colleague Detective Sergeant Sweet at West End Central Police Station to advise that you be taken into custody and charged forthwith. Do you wish to say anything further at this stage?"

"I'm glad he's dead, he was rotten. I hit him with the gas poker, not hard really, but it struck him on the temple and he went down. I panicked and set the fire. I didn't think it would take so long for me to be found."

"I would advise you not to say anything further until you are at the station and have legal counsel present." Rake stood and left the room, walking down to the telephone that sat on a table by the front door. As he dialled the woman poked her head out of her door.

"Everything alright, is it? I'm glad you got him to turn the music off, it was agitating my husband and he's got a temper."

"He's fine, Madam. Would you mind going back inside please, I have a call to make."

Rake arranged for Sweet and another officer to come and collect Fry. He requested a discreet arrest, no fuss, no nonsense. He offered to sit with Fry until they arrived. At this time of night it should be within the hour, and he thought he'd let Fry sleep, sure that silence would lead to the slumber that the man had been seeking. He went to the front door and took a step onto the path, drinking in the crisp night air, a tonic after the stuffy closeted room. He looked up at the flickering light from the window above and lit a cigarette, reflecting on the journey that had brought him here, that had brought him to this acute moment. He looked at the naked branches of a Magnolia tree in the front garden of a house across the way. It wouldn't be too long now, before it blossomed, perhaps only a month before its brief transient beauty frothed into life. Then the flowers would fall onto concrete, to be stepped over or stepped upon, laying among the dog litter and filth of another city spring.

He flicked the cigarette butt out into the gutter and walked back into the house. He climbed the stairs, weary and discontented, fighting the thought: So what? He shook it off and entered Fry's room. It took him a moment to accept what he saw, a nanosecond for the information to travel from his eyes to his brain.

Fry was still sitting in his comfortable chair. The blackness of his blouse camouflaged the blood that had soaked into its material. His throat was open, the wound circling its circumference looked to Rake like an arc of gore, an ancillary mouth. Fry's eyes opened when he heard Rake's footsteps, they opened wide, more alive than at any other time that evening, and he spoke. His words were accompanied by a bloody inundation, but Rake registered the meaning.

"I wanted a witness."

Rake strode onto the landing and bellowed down the stairwell. When the woman emerged he called for her to phone for an ambulance. Then he went to Fry and pressed his handkerchief to the wound, but it was in vain, Phillip Fry was dead.

It was well past midnight when the ambulance took the body away. Rake and Sweet walked out onto the street to let the tech boys do their job. The D.S. opened the door of the Wolsey and a halting silence arose as the erstwhile colleagues searched for something to say.

"We could give you a lift," Sweet offered finally.
Rake thought about it for a moment, then shook his head and took a step back from the car.

"You're alright, thanks Peter. You've got my statement, but if you need anything give me a ring. "

"Will do. I'll see you at the Coroners Court. I'll let you know the details."

"Fine, well Peter, good luck. I'm sorry it ended like this."

"Well, you solved the case, and that will influence your tribunal, I'm sure."

"I'm done, Peter. I'll be tendering my resignation in the morning."

"Really, you sure?"

Rake nodded, he looked up at the starless canopy of the night, it had started to rain.

"Come on," Sweet said. "You'll get soaked."

"Never mind."

"What are you going to do now?"

"I think I'll go and see Ruth."

Rake began to walk, finally pointing his body south and heading towards the river.

"Hello Vernon," Danby said.

"Hello Mister Danby."

Deeming pulled his dressing gown tightly around his body, a broad smile creasing his meaty face. He walked across to where Danby sat and plucked the Beretta from his pocket, hefting the little gun in his paw, and then he sideswiped Danby across the face with the pistol. Danby grunted, holding himself up with a stiff arm, his hand pushing into the cushion to keep from falling. He shook his head to clear it, but Deeming hit him once more, then he patted him down. Once satisfied, he went back to his seat. He sat, levelling the gun at Danby, resting his forelimb on the arm of the chair. Danby hauled himself fully upright and ran his hand through his hair. He licked at his lip and swallowed blood. He blinked to focus his eyes fully on the man sitting opposite him.

"I can't believe you thought you could stitch me up, *Harry*! Make me laugh, what? Fucking joke, you're a fucking joke, son, treacherous little toe-rag. Turn the telly on Vernon, nice and loud. Going to have some fun Harry, then it's up to Suffolk and the pigs for you."

The entry phone buzzed. Vernon and Deeming looked at one another, then Deeming nodded and Vernon slipped out of the room.

"It'll be Danieli, come crawling back. You'll see, or rather you won't. They'll all be back. See this, "Deeming spread an expansive arm around the room, "soundproofed, but you know that don't you." He stood and turned the television on, watching the screen as the set warmed up.

"Doesn't take long, not long to wait," Deeming said. Dvorak's Cello Concerto in B minor filtered onto the screen, played by the London Symphony Orchestra. "Lovely, nice bit of classical, suitable, lovely for a send off, eh Harry?" Deeming turned the volume up.

"Vernon's going to deliver the coup de grace. Keep it nice and tidy, keep him in the fold." He heard voices and turned round. Vernon came back into the room; he was followed by Alfie Atkins.

"What's this then, return of the prodigal cunt?" Vernon stepped aside; Alfie was holding the Enfield .38. He raised the revolver and fired. The bullet hit Deeming in the abdomen and he fell back into the television, knocking it crashing backwards to the floor. Music filled the room, and then there was a flash and the smell of smoke, and silence. Deeming was sitting on the rug, his back resting against the upturned television console. He looked down at his dressing gown; blood was spreading like a wine stain across the material. He tore open the gown and took in the seeping wound, blinking at it as if in mild surprise. Then he looked up and raised the Beretta, pointing it at Alfie Atkins. He hesitated momentarily, and then shifted his aim towards Danby. He pulled the trigger, the hammer clicked impotently against the firing pin. Deeming looked at the pistol in bewilderment, pointed it again and pulled the trigger several times.

"No boss," Danby said, "I emptied the magazine." He looked at Alfie Atkins and then back at Deeming. "I thought, well I thought after all, fair's fair, eh boss?"

Deeming let his arm drop to the floor, still pressing the trigger. He looked up at the three men, all now standing, looking down at him. His breathing was becoming constrained and he was sweating profusely. His mouth opened in a rictus, teeth stained with blood. He nodded.

"Fucking irons, arseholes, go on you fucking Perry's, fucking Perry Como's, think I don't know? Think I care? I don't fucking care."

Alfie took two steps forward and shot Deeming dead. The three men took the stairway down to the car park. Vernon left the Magnette where he had parked it and they separated without speaking a word, and were swallowed up by the night.

# Epilogue

## Soho London May 1960

*John Deakin left the Coach and Horses at ten past three and walked unsteadily along Romilly Street, turning onto Dean Street just as the York Minster was disgorging its lunchtime clientele onto the pavement. Deakin shouldered his way through the pack, head down, cigarette dangling from his indigo lips just by the large blister that had recently formed on the lower rim. Anonymous forms separated, shuffling into the kerb as he wended his way, until he bumped into a towering figure that remained rooted. Deakin mumbled an oath and stepped to one side, but the figure moved with him, blocking his path. It was only then that he looked up, past the barrel chest that met him at eye level, past the paisley cravat, past the Adams apple, which he noticed, had a razor nick vivid on the pale protuberance - to the eyes. The eyes were an unusual shade of blue, cerulean almost; the cornea's veined red and moist with drink, squinting under heavy blonde brows. A big meaty hand halted Deakin's progress, pressing against his concave chest, then pushing him back towards the wall and holding him there.*

    *"In a hurry jaevla rat? Where you going?" It was Viggo.*
    *"I'm going to Muriel's, I'm meeting someone."*
*Viggo shook his head. A smile creased his face. He licked his lips. He pressed harder, eased the pressure, and then he shoved Deakin roughly against the unyielding wall, knocking the air from his desiccated lungs. Deakin looked along Dean Street towards The Colony Room, he was looking for Rake, hoping for Rake, but he knew really, that Rake wasn't coming, Rake had gone and he would not be returning. Muriel Belcher had told him that Rake had briefly reconciled with Ruth, but the marriage had finally and irrevocably broken down and Rake had moved to Brighton, where he had wound up working for an insurance company, investigating claims. He missed Rake, but only like a man caught in the rain might miss his umbrella.*

*Viggo was moaning on about fifty bull's-eyes and now he was hurting him, crushing him. No one seemed to care or even notice. He was surrounded by the intoxicated, by inebriated befuddled men, all talking in loud voices, laughing loudly, doing everything that drunken people do in loud cackling empty whinnying voices, while he, Deakin, was in mortal jeopardy. The hurting intensified, his vision blurring, the landscape shifting, becoming alien to him, his sense of not belonging became all encompassing. He had tunnel vision, the periphery blurring as tears filled his eyes.*

*In that moment Viggo punched Deakin in the chest. Everything shifted as his breath left his body. He floated on the long exhalation, up through the spreading shadows, up over Dean Street towards the bleached opaqueness of the troposphere. He could see the whole street laid out before him. He could see Muriel's and Gennaro's. He could see The Caves and to his right The Golden Lion. There was Old Compton Street and Wheeler's, and David's bookshop on Greek Street. Why, he could see the whole square mile of Soho. He was a pigeon, a London pigeon, a rat with wings.*

*"What you fucking smiling at?" He heard Viggo's voice from a long way off. He imagined Viggo with a funnelled newspaper to his lips, calling from afar. Then he pictured him with a little plastic trumpet, harrumphing, stamping his big feet in a tantrum. He heard footsteps retreating, oaths being sworn in a language that he couldn't comprehend. He began to descend, to return, he could hear wings flapping about him, feathers filling his mouth, he was suffocating – and then a breath, and a cough, a gagging cough. He coughed the oily grey feathers down onto Soho. His toe touched down on concrete, but he wasn't in any particular hurry. He was going to be fine now. He could take his time.*

Printed in Great Britain
by Amazon